A TREASURY
OF STORIES
FOR
UNDER
FIVES

KINGFISHER
An imprint of Larousse plc
Elsley House, 24-30 Great Titchfield Street
London W1P 7AD

First published by Kingfisher 1994
10 9 8 7 6 5 4 3 2 1

For story acknowledgements see page 158

A CIP catalogue record for this book
is available from the British Library

ISBN 1 85697 250 X
Printed in Portugal

A TREASURY OF STORIES FOR UNDER FIVES

Chosen by
EDWARD AND NANCY BLISHEN

Illustrated by
CAROLYN DINAN

Kingfisher

CONTENTS

THE ADVENTURES OF LITTLE MOUSE

Margaret Mahy

Once a mouse family lived under the floor of a playroom. There was a mother mouse and a father mouse. There was a big sister mouse called Mousikin and a baby brother mouse called Little Mouse.

They had a pleasant mouse-hole with two doors. One door opened into a toy cupboard in the play-room. The other opened into a long hall. Mother and Father mouse ran down the long hall at night. They searched for crumbs or went into the kitchen to steal cheese. Mousikin and Little Mouse were not allowed to run in the hall. However, Mousikin was sometimes allowed to go into the toy cupboard. Little Mouse was too small to go anywhere. How he longed to see the world outside!

"What is the world like, Mousikin?" he would ask. "Is it strange? Is it exciting? What smells are there in the world, Mousikin?"

"It is very strange out in the world, Little Mouse," said Mousikin. "The world is a lot of shelves one on top of the other. On the shelves are soft, staring creatures with round eyes. They do not blink or wink or even see anything. They don't smile or twitch their whiskers. They just sit there. They are called toys. There is a striped box, and if you open that box out leaps a little striped man – bang! And he grins at you. He is called Jack-in-the-box. There is a round red ball that would roll and bounce if there was room. There are blocks too. You can make mouse castles with them. The world smells of dust and rubber and books."

"What are books, Mousikin?"

"Books are all sizes and colours, Little Mouse. You turn the pages. You look at the pictures. You grow wise and clever."

"What does it mean to be wise, Mousikin?"

"It means to know all sorts of things, Little Mouse. It means to know why cheese smells so nice and how to tie a bell round the neck of a cat. It means to know how to bake bread or sing a song, or to know where sugar comes from."

"Is it good to be wise, Mousikin?"

"It is the best thing in the world, Little Mouse. That is why I am teaching myself to read. I can read 'A is for Apple, B is for Bear'. I can read long words too."

Little Mouse thought for a moment.

"Will you tell me the new words you learn, Mousikin? Then I will be wise too. I will be the wisest Little Mouse in the world."

So Mousikin would come back from the toy cupboard and tell Little Mouse the new words she had learnt. Little Mouse learned 'A for Apple, B for Bear' too. He liked the long words best.

"What long words Little Mouse is saying now," said Father Mouse proudly.

Brontosaurus

Then one day Mousikin came back from the toy
cupboard, her black eyes round and shining.

"Oh, Little Mouse! Do you know what I saw today in
the toy cupboard? I saw a picture in a book, Little Mouse.
It was a picture of a huge monster, bigger than a cat,
bigger than a dog . . . bigger even than a rocking-horse.
Its name was the longest in the world. Its name – listen
carefully, Little Mouse – its name was Brontosaurus."

Little Mouse twitched his whiskers.

"Brontosaurus!" he said. "That word is longer than I am."

"It means Thunder Lizard, Little Mouse. This monster was so big it was called the Thunder Lizard. It had a long, long neck and a teeny-tiny head. It had a great fat body and stumpy legs. Behind it was a tail as long as its neck."

"Was its tail longer than my tail, Mousikin?" asked Little Mouse, who thought he had a very long tail indeed.

"Of course it was, you foolish Little Mouse. Its tail was longer than yours, longer than mine. It was longer than a piece of string. It was the tail of a monster."

Little Mouse dreamed of the monster called Brontosaurus. He said its name over and over to himself. For two whole days he did not think of anything else but the Brontosaurus. He thought of its long neck and its teeny-tiny head. He thought of its tail.

"Brontosaurus means Thunder Lizard," said Little Mouse to himself. He began to think of seeing the picture of the Brontosaurus for himself. "I would like to see the picture of that Brontosaurus."

Little Mouse asked to go to the toy cupboard with Mousikin.

"No, no, Little Mouse!" said his mother. "You are too small."

"If someone opened the cupboard door you would not know where to run to," said Father Mouse. "Children would catch you and put you in a cage. When you are older you can go with Mousikin."

Little Mouse said nothing. He was making a special Little Mouse plan to go on his own, when no one was looking.

Next day when his parents were away and Mousikin was asleep Little Mouse stole out on his own. He wanted to get to the toy cupboard but he did not know the way. Down a dark passage he went, his whiskers prickling with excitement. He did not know where he was going. It was not the passage to the toy cupboard – it was the passage to the hall.

As he went Little Mouse heard a roar like thunder. Could it be a Brontosaurus roaring somewhere? He listened carefully. Then he went on very slowly. He came to the mouse-hole and peeped out. The mouse-hole was behind a big black chest in the hall. No one could see Little Mouse, but Little Mouse could see everything that was going on. The first thing he saw was a Brontosaurus.

Little Mouse knew it was a Brontosaurus because it had a long snaky neck and teeny-tiny head. It had a black tail too – a long, long tail. It was the longest tail Little Mouse had ever seen.

Someone was taking the Brontosaurus for a walk.

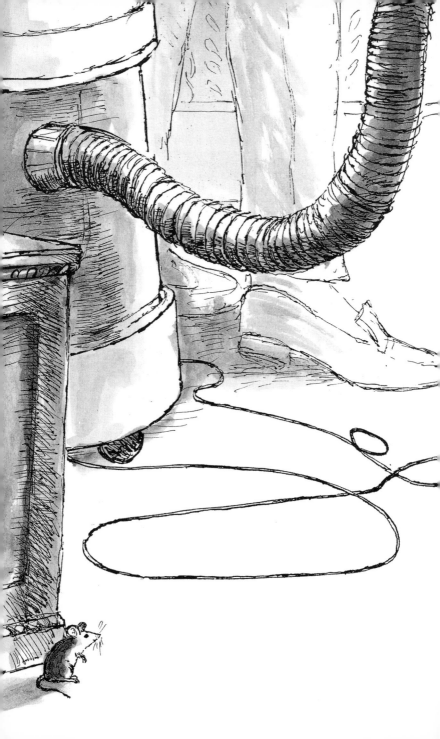

Little Mouse could see a pair of feet walking beside it and a hand on its shiny neck. Its teeny-tiny head was flat on the ground. As it went by it roared like thunder and sucked up the dust. "The Brontosaurus is a Thunder Lizard," whispered Little Mouse softly. The whole world shook as the Brontosaurus went by.

Down at the end of the hall a door opened. Someone called out, "Will you be much longer?"

"No," said the owner of the feet that were taking the Brontosaurus for a walk. "I will just put the vacuum cleaner away." Someone picked the Brontosaurus up, and unplugged its tail from the wall. Someone carried the Brontosaurus away.

Little Mouse scurried back home down the mouse passage. How surprised his parents and Mousikin would be to hear how brave he had been.

"Mousikin, Mousikin! I have seen a real one. It is bigger than we ever thought and it really roars like thunder. Not only that, Mousikin, it eats dirt and dust for its tea. I saw it, Mousikin – and, Mousikin, it has another name. It is called Vacuum Cleaner."

"Oh, Little Mouse!" said Mousikin. "How wise you are now."

"Yes," said Father Mouse, "but he should not have run away like that. Tomorrow you can go to the toy cupboard with Mousikin, but you must never go to the hall again. The Brontosaurus might get you next time."

Little Mouse twitched his whiskers.

"Are you pleased, Little Mouse? Are you happy?" asked Mousikin.

Little Mouse smiled a mouse smile.

"I am so happy I feel as if all the world was cheese," he said. And so he was.

MY NAUGHTY LITTLE SISTER GOES TO THE PANTOMIME

Dorothy Edwards

A long time ago, when I was a little girl, and my little sister was a little girl too, my mother took us to see the Christmas Pantomime.

The Pantomime was in a Theatre, which was a very beautiful place with red tippy-up seats and a lot of ladies and gentlemen playing music in front of the curtains.

My little sister was a very good quiet child at first, because she had never been to the Pantomime before. She sat very still and mousy. She didn't say anything. She just looked and looked.

She looked at the lights, and the lots and lots of seats, and the music people and the other boys and girls. She didn't even fidget at first, because she wasn't quite sure about the tippy-up seat.

When we were in the Theatre, our mother gave us a bag of sweets each. I had chocolate-creams, and my little sister had toffee-drops, because she liked them so much, but she was so quiet that she didn't eat even a single one of them before the Pantomime started.

She just held the sweeties on her lap, so that when the music man who plays the cymbals suddenly made them go "Rish-tish a-tish!" and the curtains came back, she was so surprised that she dropped them all over the floor, and my mother had to pick them up for her.

My little sister was so surprised because she hadn't known that Pantomime was people dancing and singing and falling over things, but when she saw that it was, she was very excited, and when the other children clapped their hands, she clapped hers very hard too.

At first, my little sister was so surprised that she liked every bit of it, but after a while she said her favourite was the fat funny man. The play was all about the Babes in the Wood, and the fat funny man was called Humpty Dumpty. He was very funny indeed, and when he came on, he always said, "Hallo, boys and girls."

And the boys and girls said, "Hallo, Humpty Dumpty."

And he said, "How are you tomorrow?" and we said, "We are very well today." He told us to say this every time, and we never forgot. Once, my little sister shouted so loud, "*Hallo, Humpty Dumpty.*" She shouted, "HALLO, HUMPTY DUMPTY," like that, that Humpty Dumpty heard her, and he waved specially to her. My goodness, wasn't she a proud girl then!

16

The other thing my little sister liked was the fairies dancing. There were lots of fairies in the Pantomime, and they had lovely sparkly dresses, and when they danced the lights went red and blue and green, and some of them *really flew* right up in the air!

Humpty Dumpty tried to fly too, but he fell right over and bumped his nose. My naughty little sister was so sorry for him, that she began to cry and cry, really true tear-crying, not just howling.

But when Humpty Dumpty jumped up and said, "Hallo, boys and girls," and we all said, "Hallo, Humpty Dumpty," and when he began to dance again, she knew he wasn't really hurt so she laughed and laughed.

And presently, what do you think? My little sister had a really exciting thing happen.

Humpty Dumpty came on to the stage and he sang a little song for all the boys and girls, and then he made all the children sing too. After that he said, "Would any little boy or girl like to come up on the stage and dance with me?" And do you know what my little sister said? "Yes, I will. I will." And she ran out of her seat and up the stage steps and right on to the big theatre stage before my mother could do anything about it.

All the people cheered and clapped when my little sister ran up on to the stage, and a lot of other boys and girls went up too then, and soon they were all dancing with Humpty Dumpty. Round and round and up and down, until two ladies dressed like men came on the stage.

Then Humpty Dumpty said, "All right, children, down you go," and all the boys and girls went down again, off the stage and back to their mothers.

All except my bad little sister. *Because she wasn't there.* She'd vanished! And what do you think?

While the two ladies dressed like men were singing on the stage, the funny man came back, with my little sister sitting on his shoulder. And he came right off the stage and down the steps and brought her back to mother, and my little sister looked very pleased and smily.

All the people stared and stared to see my naughty little sister being carried back by Humpty Dumpty. Even the singing ladies dressed like men stared.

And do you know where she had been?

The bad child had slipped round the side of the stage while the other children were dancing, to see if she could find the fairies!

And she did find them too. She said they were drinking lemonade and they gave her some as well. It wasn't very fairyish lemonade, she said, it was the fizzy nose-tickle sort.

She told us another thing too, a secret thing. She said they weren't real true fairies, only little girls like herself, and she said that when she was a bit older she was going to be a stage fairy like those little girls.

FIVE

Barbara Sleigh

Once upon a time, an old witch lived in Jamaica. She can't have been a very clever witch, or she would have magicked herself a much better home than the tumbledown hut she lived in. But there it is. Some people are good at one thing and some at another.

Everyone called her just "Five". She had been called "Five" since the oldest grandmother could remember. Nobody knew why. Perhaps because it was safer to hold up five fingers and nod in the direction of her hut, instead of saying her name out loud. You never know with witches.

The old woman hated being called just "Five". "Why can't I have a proper name like everyone else?" she grumbled angrily. "Five! Why, it doesn't even *mean* a name like Mandy or Poll. I shall make a magic such as no one has ever made before, to stop anyone calling me Five again."

Now it happened that just then Anansi came along. Anansi was a magic person himself. Sometimes he was a man, and sometimes he was a spider, but whichever it was, there was always mischief afoot when he was about.

When Anansi came to the witch's hut, he said to himself, "I wonder what old Five is up to now?" And he peeked through a hole in the wall of the tumbledown house. (Mind you, Anansi was the sort who would *make* a hole in the wall of your house if it suited him.) What should he see but the old witch lighting a fire under her cooking pot and dropping all kinds of horrid things into it. Some were pink and slimy: some had legs, and some were so nasty I don't like to tell you what they were. Well, when she had got the cooking pot full to the brim and bubbling, she screeched out a terrible strong spell, that anyone who said the word "Five" should drop down dead.

When Anansi heard this, he chuckled to himself. "This magic is going to be mighty useful for me and my hungry wife and family!" And he tiptoed quietly away.

Next morning he filled a great sack full of yams. (Yams are round and knobbly, like potatoes.) And he heaped them in five piles by the side of the path that everyone used on the way to market. And then he sat down and waited. Presently, along came Mrs Turkey. "Gibble gubble! Gibble gubble!" Very fat, and high and mighty she was.

"Mrs Turkey, dear Mrs Turkey," said Anansi. "Just the very person I hoped I should meet, for I know how clever you are, and how very kind!"

"What can I do to help you, Mr Anansi?" said Mrs Turkey, fluffing out her feathers in a grand way.

"Well," said Anansi humbly, "it's like this. I've grown these fine yams, and made them into piles for folks to buy

on their way to market, and I'm blessed if I haven't
forgotten how to count them!"

"Gibble gubble! Gibble gubble! Nothing could be
easier!" said Mrs Turkey, looking down her beak at
wicked old Anansi, and she began to count, "One-gibble,
two-gubble, three-gibble, four-gubble . . ." but of course
the minute she said "five", she dropped down dead, and
Anansi gobbled her up, every bit, and didn't leave a scrap
for his hungry wife and family.

He had only just wiped his mouth and hidden away
the feathers, when along came kind Mrs Duck, waddle
waddle, "Quack, quack!"

"Oh, Mrs Duck dear," said Anansi. "Will you be so good and kind as to count my piles of yams for me? I've quite forgotten how to do it."

"Quack, quack, of course!" said Mrs Duck. "Anything to help a friend." And she began to count, "One heap, two heaps, three heaps, four heaps..." And of course the minute she said "five" she dropped down dead, and Anansi gobbled her up, every bit. And still he didn't leave a scrap for his hungry wife and family.

He had just wiped his mouth, and hidden all the feathers, feeling rather uncomfortable inside because he had eaten so much, when along came Mrs Dove, pretty, silly Mrs Dove, with her pink feet and snow-white feathers. "Coo-roo, coo-roo!" said pretty Mrs Dove. "Of course I'll count your piles of yams for you." She fluttered up on top of the first heap. "One!" she cooed: and fluttered up on to the next: "Two!" she cooed, "And three

– and four . . ." But when she fluttered on to the top of the last heap, she said, "And the one I am sitting on!"

"That isn't right at all!" said Anansi crossly, for he was feeling very uncomfortable inside because he had eaten so much. "Count them again!"

So Mrs Dove fluttered back on to the first pile once more. "One!" she cooed. "And two! And three! And four! . . . And the one I am sitting on!"

"You silly, stupid Mrs Dove! You don't know how to count at all!" shouted Anansi. And because his too-full inside was hurting so, he quite forgot about the witch's spell, and he bawled out, "It's one, two, three, four, FIVE!"

And of course, as soon as he said "five", *he* dropped down dead.

And Mrs Dove flew down from the last pile of yams, and went hopping on to market on her pretty pink feet.

THE LITTLE BRUTE FAMILY

Russell Hoban

I n the middle of a dark and shadowy wood lived a little family of Brutes. There were Papa Brute, Mama Brute, Brother and Sister Brute, and Baby Brute.

In the morning Mama cooked a sand and gravel porridge, and the family snarled and grimaced as they spooned it up.

No one said, "Please." No one said, "Thank you," and no one said, "How delicious," because it was not delicious.

Baby Brute howled between spoonfuls. Brother and Sister kicked each other under the table, and Mama and Papa made faces while they ate.

After breakfast Papa Brute took up his sack and went off to gather sticks and stones. Mama stayed home to thump the furniture and bang the pots and scold the baby. And Brother and Sister pushed and shoved and punched and pinched their way to school.

In the evenings Mama served a stew of sticks and stones, and the family ate it with growls and grumbling.

Then they groaned and went to sleep.

That was how they lived.

They never laughed and said, "Delightful!"
They never smiled and said, "How lovely!"
In the spring the little Brutes made heavy kites that
bumped along the ground and would not fly.

In the summer they flung themselves into the pond
and sank like stones but never learned to swim.

In the autumn they jumped into great piles of leaves and stamped on one another, yelling.

In the winter they leaped upon their crooked clumsy sleds that took them crashing into snowbanks where they stuck headfirst and screamed.

That was how they lived in the dark and shadowy woods.

Then one day Baby Brute found a little wandering lost good feeling in a field of daisies, and he caught it in his paw and put it in his tiny pocket.

And he felt so good that he laughed and said, "How lovely."

Baby Brute felt good all afternoon, and at supper when his bowl was filled with stew he said, "Thank you."

Then the little good feeling flew out of his tiny pocket and hovered over the table, humming and smiling.

"How lovely!" said Mama, without even snarling.

"Delightful!" said Papa, forgetting to growl.

"Oh, please," said all the little Brutes together, "let it stay with us!"

And Papa smiled and said, "All right."

When Papa Brute went out for sticks and stones the next day, he found wild berries, salad greens, and honey, and he brought them home instead.

At supper everyone said, "How delicious!" because it *was* delicious, and everyone said, "Please" and "Thank you." And they never ate stick and stone stew again.

Then the little good feeling stopped wandering and stayed with the little Brute family.

When springtime came the little Brutes made bright new kites that flew high in the sky, and in the summer they swam beautifully.

In the autumn they gathered nuts and acorns that they roasted by a cosy fire when winter came.

And in the evening they sang songs together.

The little good feeling stayed and stayed and never went away, and when springtime came again the little Brute family changed their name to Nice.

LITTLE DOG TURPIE

Leila Berg

Once upon a time there was a little old man and a little old woman, and they lived together in a little old house with their Little Dog Turpie.

Now out in the woods lived the Hobyahs. Every night they came running towards the house, up, up, on their long toes, creeping, creeping, through the soft grass, waving their wild tails, came the Hobyahs. And they shouted, "Break down the house, carry off the little old man, eat up the little old woman!" But Little Dog Turpie always heard them coming, and he would bark and bark and bark, "Wow, wow!" till they all ran away.

The little old man and the little old woman didn't know about the Hobyahs, because Little Dog Turpie always frightened them away. But one night the old man sat up in bed and said, "Little Dog Turpie barks so loudly that I can't sleep. In the morning I shall take off his tail."

So in the morning the little old man took off Little Dog Turpie's tail because he barked so much.

That night when the old man and the old woman were in bed, out of the woods came the Hobyahs. Up, up, on their long toes, creeping, creeping, through the soft

32

grass, waving their wild tails, came the Hobyahs. And they shouted, "Break down the house, carry off the little old man, eat up the little old woman!" But Little Dog Turpie heard them coming and he barked and he barked and he barked, "Wow, wow!" till they ran away.

But the little old man sat up in bed and said, "Little Dog Turpie barks too loudly, and I can't sleep. In the morning I shall take off his legs."

So in the morning the little old man took off Little Dog Turpie's legs, because he barked so much.

The next night, when the little old man and the little old woman were in bed, out of the woods came the Hobyahs. Up, up, on their long toes, creeping, creeping, through the soft grass, waving their wild tails, came the Hobyahs. And they shouted, "Break down the house, carry off the little old man, eat up the little old woman!" But Little Dog Turpie heard them coming, and he barked and barked and barked, till they all ran away.

But the little old man sat up in bed and said, "That Little Dog Turpie barks too loudly, and I can't get any sleep. In the morning I shall take off his head."

So in the morning the little old man took off Little
Dog Turpie's head.

That night, when the little old man and the little old
woman were in bed, out of the woods came the Hobyahs.
Up, up, on their long toes, creeping, creeping through
the soft grass, waving their wild tails came the Hobyahs.
And they shouted, "Break down the house, carry off the
little old man, eat up the little old woman!" And Little
Dog Turpie felt them coming, but the little old man had
taken off his head, and now he couldn't bark any more
and frighten them away.

So the Hobyahs broke down the house. They didn't
carry off the little old man, because he hid under the
kitchen table and they couldn't find him. But they
carried off the little old woman to their Hobyah house,
and they put her in a bag and hung her on the door-
knob.

When the little old man found the Hobyahs had
carried off the little old woman, he was very sorry for
what he had done. Now he knew why Little Dog Turpie
had been barking every night. "I am a silly old man," he
said. "I shall put back Little Dog Turpie's tail and his feet

and his head this very minute." So he went out into the yard and put them all back right away.

Then Little Dog Turpie went running off on his four legs to find the little old woman. He ran and he ran till he came to the Hobyah house. The Hobyahs were not at home, but they had left the little old woman hanging in the bag on the door-knob. Little Dog Turpie bit the bag with his sharp teeth till it fell off the door-knob, and then he pulled it open so that the little old woman could get out. She ran all the way back home to the little old man, and they were very pleased to see each other again, I can tell you, and they had a bit of a kiss and a hug.

But Little Dog Turpie crept inside the bag himself, and lay there waiting for the Hobyahs to come home again. Presently they came, and the first thing they did was to poke the bag with their long fingers, for they thought it was the old woman, you see. And out jumped Little Dog Turpie, barking as loudly as he could. The Hobyahs got such a fright they all ran away, and they ran so far they never came back. And that's why there are no Hobyahs today, not one.

A BED FOR TINY TED

Margaret Joy

There was once a boy called William who *loved* teddy bears. He had so many, that there wasn't room for them in bed beside him – they all slept on their own special pillow at the bottom of William's bed. When he was tucked up in bed, he could stretch his toes down and wriggle them about and feel the furry toes of his bears.

First there was soft orange-coloured Bear-Bear; then there was big brown Grandad Bear, who was rather fat and made a noise like this if you pressed his tummy: Aaaaaaaakkk! Then there were the twin bears, Teddy and Freddy, one twin was green with a blue ribbon, and the other twin was blue with a green ribbon.

Every night before he got into bed, William would arrange his bears on their own special pillow, pull the bedclothes up over their furry tummies and tuck them in.

When his mother came to tuck William up, she would look at the bears on their pillow, and shake her head.

"There's *just* enough room for all your bears, William," she would say. "What *will* you do if you get another bear? There won't be any room for it!"

"Oh, I'll think of something," said William.

Then, some weeks later, another bear did come to live with them. It happened like this.

William and his mother went to a Jumble Sale. Most of the jumble sale tables were covered with clothes which weren't very interesting, but there was one table in a corner with all sorts of odd bits and pieces on it. William went to look at them.

"There's an umbrella, a vase and some books and a necklace and a teapot and a jar of jam," cried William. Then he said: "Oh, Mummy – just *see* what's peeping out from behind that teapot!"

"Well I never!" said his mother. "It's a tiny teddy bear!"

"I should like to buy it," William said to the jumble sale lady. "I've got four pence, will that be enough?"

"That's exactly right," said the jumble sale lady. "The bear costs four pence." And she took William's money and gave him the tiny bear.

If you hold out your hand, you'll see how big that bear was: just as big as the palm of your hand. He was knitted in bright red wool and had two black eyes and a big black smile.

"Oh, he's a lovely bear!" said William. "And he's so tiny! I'll call him Tiny Ted."

When it was bedtime that evening, William took Tiny Ted upstairs. He got undressed and put on his pyjamas, then he tucked up all his other bears on their special pillow.

"Goodnight Bear-Bear, goodnight Grandad Bear, goodnight Teddy and Freddy!" he said.

His mother came into the bedroom and shook her head: "There's just not room on that pillow for Tiny Ted – where's *he* going to sleep?"

"I've got a sleeping bag for him," said William.

"A sleeping bag?" said his mother, surprised, looking all round. "Where?"

"Here!" said William, pointing to the pocket on the front of his pyjamas. "See, it's just like a sleeping bag!"

And he tucked Tiny Ted right down into his pocket so that only his little black eyes peeped out over the top.

"He fits perfectly!" said William. "So he can sleep with me, and if I wake in the night, I'll have someone to talk to!"

THE THIN KING AND THE FAT COOK

Donald Bisset

Once upon a time there was a very fat King who said to his very thin cook, "Bake me a cake! The lightest, nicest, scrumpiest cake you've ever made."

So the cook got a big bowl and two dozen eggs and some butter and five pounds of flour and a pound of yeast.

He mixed the flour and the eggs and the butter in the big bowl, then put in the yeast. Then he lit the gas and when the oven was hot he put the cake in.

Soon there was a lovely smell of baking cake, and the King came running in.

"My, my!" he said. "What a lovely smell. I'm sure it's going to be a delicious cake, cook."

"Ah, yes, Your Majesty," said the cook, "and it's going to be the lightest cake in the world. I put in a whole pound of yeast to make it rise."

"That's the stuff!" said the King. "But what's this?" They looked round and saw that the top of the gas stove was beginning to bend and suddenly, with a *Crack!* it shot up in the air and the top of the cake appeared, rising slowly.

"Tch, tch!" said the King. "Now, look what you've done! You put in *too much* yeast!"

The cake went on rising until, at last, it was pressing against the ceiling, which began to crack.

The cook and the King rushed upstairs and when they got to the top they saw the cake had gone right through the ceiling to the floor above.

"Do something, my good man!" shouted the King. The poor cook didn't know what to do. So he jumped up and sat on the cake to stop it rising.

But it went on rising just the same till the cook felt his head bump on the ceiling. A moment later his head went through the roof and still the cake went on rising.

"Oh, Your Majesty! Please go and turn the gas off!" shouted the cook.

The King rushed downstairs and turned the gas off. Then he got his telescope and went into the garden.

The cake had stopped rising, but the top was very high up in the air.

"Oh, drat the man!" said the King. "If he doesn't come down soon there won't be anyone to cook dinner." Then he thought, "If the cook was to start eating the cake, then he would get lower and lower." So he called out, "Cook, eat the cake, at once!"

"Delighted, Your Majesty," called back the cook, and he took a bite. "Yum, yum!" he said. "This *is* nice cake!"

"Oh, stop talking," said the King, "and eat it up as fast as you can, or I shall have no dinner."

"Right, Your Majesty," said the cook, and ate as fast as he could. But it was such a big cake that it took him two weeks to eat it all and it made him very fat. But the poor King, who was waiting for his dinner, got thinner and thinner.

So instead of the King being fat and the cook being thin, there was a very thin King and a very fat cook!

"Never mind, Your Majesty," called the cook when he had eaten the cake and reached the ground. "I'll cook you a lovely dinner now!" And he did.

ONE
VERY
SMALL
FOOT

Dick King-Smith

"What animal has got only one foot?" said the children's father. "I bet you can't tell me."

"I can!" said Matthew and Mark with one voice. As well as looking exactly alike, the twins nearly always said exactly the same thing at exactly the same time. Matthew was ten minutes older than Mark, but after that there had never been the slightest difference between them.

"Go on then," said their father. "Tell me. What animal's got only one foot?"

"A chicken standing on one leg!" they said.

"That's silly," said Sophie seriously.

Sophie was four, a couple of years younger than her brothers.

"That's silly," she said. "It would still have a foot on the other leg. Anyway, Daddy, there isn't really an animal that's only got one foot, is there?"

"Yes, there is, Sophie."

"What?"

"A snail. Every snail has a big flat sticky muscle under it that it travels along on. That's called its foot. Next

43

time you see a snail crawling along, pick it up carefully and turn it over, and you'll see. There are loads in the garden."

"Come on! Let's find one!" said Matthew to Mark and Mark to Matthew at the same time.

"Wait for me," said Sophie. But they didn't, so she plodded after them.

When she caught up with the twins, in a far corner of the garden, each was examining the underside of a large snail. Sophie was not surprised to see that the snails were also obviously twins, the same size, the same shape, the same striped greeny-browny colour.

"I know!" said Matthew.

"I know what you're going to say!" said Mark.

"Let's have a snail race!" they said.

"How are you going to tell them apart?" said Sophie.

"I know!" said Mark.

"I know what you're going to say!" said Matthew.

"Fetch us a felt pen, Sophie," they said.

"What are you going to do?" asked Sophie when she came back with a red felt pen.

"Put my initial on my snail," said Mark and Matthew together.

"But you've got the same initial."

The boys looked at each other.

"I know!" they said.

"I know what you're going to say," said Sophie, and she plodded off again. She came back with a blue felt pen.

After a moment, "Ready?" said Matthew, holding up his snail with a big red M on its shell, and at the same instant, "Ready?" said Mark, holding up his snail with a big blue M.

"Wait for me," said Sophie. "I haven't got a snail yet," but already the twins had set their twin snails side by side on the path that ran between the edge of the lawn and the flowerbed. The path was made of big oval flagstones, and they chose the largest one, perhaps a metre long. The far end of the flagstone was to be the winning-post.

"Ready, steady, go!" they shouted.

Sophie plodded off. "I'll beat them," she said. She was small but very determined.

Behind the first stone she moved, almost as though it had been waiting for her, was a snail. It was as different as possible from Red M and Blue M. It was very little, no bigger than Sophie's middle fingernail, and it was a lovely buttercup yellow.

As she watched, it stretched out its head, poked out its two horns, and began to crawl, very slowly. It had a most intelligent face, Sophie thought. She picked it up carefully, and turned it over.

"What a very small-sized shoe you would take, my dear," she said. "I don't know whether you can win a race but you are very beautiful. You shall be my snail."

"Who won?" she said to Matthew and Mark when she returned.

"They didn't go the right way," they both said.

"But mine went furthest," they both said.

"No it didn't," they both said.

They picked up their snails and put them side by side once more.

"Wait for me," Sophie said, and she put down the little yellow snail. It looked very small beside the others.

"Just look at Sophie's snail!" hooted the twins, but this time when they shouted "Ready, steady, go!" neither

Red M nor Blue M would move. They stayed stubbornly inside their shells and took not the slightest notice of their owners' cries of encouragement.

Sophie's snail plodded off.

It was small but very determined, and Sophie lay on the grass beside the path and watched it putting its best foot forward.

After half an hour, it reached the winning-post.

Sophie jumped up. "Mine's the winner!" she cried, but there was no one to hear. The twins had become bored with snail-racing at exactly the same time and gone away. Red M and Blue M had gone away too, into the forest of the flowerbed. Only Sophie's snail kept stoutly on, while the straight silvery trail it had left glistened in the sunshine.

Sophie knelt down and carefully put her hand flat in front of the little yellow creature. It crawled solemnly onto it.

"You have such an intelligent look, my dear," said Sophie.

"What *have* you got in your hand, Sophie?" said her mother at tea-time.

"It's Sophie's snail!" chorused Matthew and Mark.

"Put it straight out in the garden," said the children's mother.

"No," said Sophie in a small but determined voice.

Her mother looked at her, sighed, picked up a box of matches, emptied the matches out and gave Sophie the empty box.

"Put it in there till after tea," she said, " and go and wash your hands."

All that evening Sophie played with her snail. When it was bedtime, and she was ready to wash and do her teeth, she put the snail carefully on the flat rim of the washbasin.

Then (as she always did) she filled the basin with warm water right up to the overflow and washed her face and hands. The snail did not move, though it appeared to be watching.

Then (as she always did) she

brushed her teeth very hard, making a lot of froth in her mouth and spitting the bubbly blobs of toothpaste out on top of the rather dirty water. She always liked doing this. The toothpaste blobs made strange shapes on the surface of the water, often like a map of the world. Tonight there was a big white Africa at one side of the basin.

Then (as she always did) she pulled the plug out, but as she turned to dry her hands the sleeve of her dressing gown scuffed the rim of the basin. Right into the middle of disappearing Africa fell a small yellow shape, and then the last of the whirlpooling frothing water disappeared down the plug hole, leaving the basin quite empty.

Sophie plodded down the stairs.

"My snail's gone down the plug hole," she said in a very quiet voice.

"You couldn't have kept it, you know," said her father gently. "It would have died anyway without its natural food."

"Next time you find one," said her mother, "just leave it in the garden. There are lots of other snails there, just as nice."

"Not as nice as my snail," said Sophie. She looked so unhappy that for once the twins said different things, in an effort to comfort her.

" 'Spect it died quickly," said Matthew.

"Sure to be drowned by now," said Mark.

Try as she would, Sophie could not stop herself thinking about what happened to you if you went down a plug hole. She lay in bed and thought about the twins washing their hands in the basin and washing their teeth, and then later on Mum and Dad doing the same. All that water would be washing the body of her snail farther and farther away, down the drain into the sewer, down the sewer into the river, down the river into the sea.

When at last she slept, she dreamed that she was walking by the seaside, and there she saw, washed up on the beach, a familiar little yellow shape. But when she ran and picked it up, it had no head, no horns, no foot. It was just an empty snail shell.

Sophie woke early with the feeling that something awful had happened, and then she remembered what it was.

She plodded along to the bathroom and looked over the rim of the washbasin at the round plug hole with its metal grating meant to stop things going down it.

"But you were too small," she said.

Leaning over as far as she could reach, she stared sadly into the black depths of the plug hole. And as she stared,

suddenly two little horns poked up through the grating, and then a head, and then a shell no bigger than her middle fingernail, a shell that was a lovely buttercup yellow.

Very carefully Sophie reached out and picked up her small determined snail.

Very quietly she plodded down the stairs and opened the back door and went out into the garden and crossed the dewy lawn.

Very gently, at the exact spot she had found it, she put her snail down and watched it slowly move away on its very small foot.

"Goodbye, my dear," said Sophie. "I hope we meet again," and then she sat happily on the wet grass watching, till at last there was nothing more to be seen of Sophie's snail.

HORACE

Alice B. Coats

Once upon a time there was a family who all lived
together in a little house in a wood. There was
Great-Grandpa,
Great-Grandma,
Grandpa,
Grandma,
Pa,
Ma,
Paul,
and little Lulu.
And with them lived HORACE.
Horace was a bear!

One day, Pa went out hunting, and on the way
back he was met by

Great-Grandma,

Grandpa,

Grandma,

Ma,

Paul,

and little Lulu.

And they all said, "What do you think has
happened?"

And Pa said, "What *has* happened?"

And they said, "Horace has eaten Great-Grandpa!"

And Pa was just WILD, and
he said, "I will KILL Horace!"

But they all took on so, he
hadn't the heart to do it.

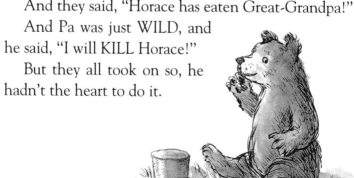

And the next day, Pa went out hunting, and on the way
back he was met by

Grandpa,

Grandma,

Ma,

Paul,

and little Lulu.

And they all said, "What do you think has
happened?"

And Pa said, "What *has* happened?"

And they said, "Horace has eaten Great-Grandma!"

And Pa was just WILD, and he said, "I will KILL
Horace!"

But they all took on so, he
hadn't the heart to do it.

And the next day, Pa went out hunting, and on the way back he was met by

Grandma,

Ma,

Paul,

and little Lulu.

And they all said, "What do you think has happened?"

And Pa said, "What *has* happened?"

And they said, "Horace has eaten Grandpa!"

And Pa was just WILD, and he said, "I will KILL Horace!"

But they all took on so, he hadn't the heart to do it.

And the next day, Pa went out hunting, and on the way back he was met by

Ma,

Paul,

and little Lulu.

And they all said, "What do you think has happened?"

And Pa said, "What *has* happened?"

And they said, "Horace has eaten Grandma!"

And Pa was just WILD, and he said, "I will KILL Horace!"

But they all took on so, he hadn't the heart to do it.

And the next day, Pa went out
hunting, and on the way back he was
met by
    Paul,
    and little Lulu.
    And they both said, "What do
you think has happened?"
    And Pa said, "What *has*
happened?"
    And they said, "Horace has
eaten Ma!"
    And Pa was just WILD, and he said, "I will KILL
Horace!"
    But they all took on so, he hadn't the heart to do it.

And the next day, Pa went out hunting, and on the way
back he was met by little Lulu.
    And little Lulu said, "What do you think has
happened?"
    And Pa said, "What *has* happened?"
    And little Lulu said, "Horace has eaten Paul!"
    And Pa was just WILD, and he said, "I will KILL
Horace!"
    But little Lulu took on so, he hadn't the heart to do it.

And the next day, Pa went out hunting, and on the way back he was met by Horace.

And Horace said, "What do you think has happened?"

And Pa said, "What *has* happened?"

And Horace said, "I've eaten little Lulu!"

And Pa was just WILD, and he said, "I will kill you, Horace!"

But Horace took on so, he hadn't the heart to do it.

And the next day, Horace went out hunting.

THE EASTER SURPRISE

Nancy Blishen

Michael and Jenny were twins. They lived with their mother and father in a house on the edge of town. There was only a tiny garden, so one of their biggest treats was to go and stay with Nana and Grandpa, who lived in the country and whose garden was huge. It had trees, and it had secret places to hide in. There was a swing for each of them, and Grandpa had built a tree house that you could reach only by climbing a rope ladder.

So imagine their delight when one morning their mother opened a letter, read it and said: "Well, listen to this! Nana has invited you for Easter, and she thinks that now you are nearly five, and are grown up, you might like to stay there on your own? What do you say?"

"Oh, yes," said Michael. "Grandpa always spoils us when we are there by ourselves, even just for a day!"

"And Nana makes surprises and special treats," said Jenny. "And it's Easter!"

What she meant was, there would be Easter eggs – lots of them!

And so it was that on Easter morning the twins found themselves in their pretty bedroom at Nana's house. The thing they liked best about that room was what they called the treasure chest. It was in a corner of the room, and it was full of toys. Some of them – like an old-fashioned fire engine and a baker's van – had belonged to Grandpa when he was a boy. And Jenny's favourites were the very small wooden dolls Nana's mummy had dressed for *her* when she was little.

The twins had made tents of their bedclothes and were giggling inside them when they heard Grandpa coming up the stairs. He opened the door and in the cross and growly voice that was only a pretend voice he said: "Now, you big-eared, flat-footed, knock-kneed, scatterbrained pair of scoundrels, up you get on this sunny Easter morning!" And though they knew it was going to happen, when he pulled the bedclothes off, the twins giggled so much that they rolled off the beds and onto the floor.

When they got down to breakfast Nana was cooking porridge. The children loved that because they were allowed to sprinkle brown sugar on it, and each had a tiny silver jug of cream. *Cream!* That was one of Nana's treats. And from the oven came a lovely smell of . . .

They sniffed and sniffed. What was it?

Of course! Hot cross buns!

But oh dear! Something was missing. Oh dear! Oh dear!

No Easter eggs!

Usually the eggs were on the table beside their plates. But this year – nothing! Michael's lip began to tremble, but Jenny whispered: "Never mind, Mikey – maybe Nana forgot. Just think of the hot cross buns we're going to have in a moment!" But then there was a scratching at the back door and a miaowing. "I think Mitzi wants to come in. Will you go and open the back door for me, please, Mikey," said Grandpa.

So Michael got up and opened the door to let the cat in, and he was just closing it again when he happened to look down the garden.

"Jenny," he cried. "Come and see!"

In the branches of nearly every tree there were . . . *eggs!*

Eggs of all colours and sizes! The twins jumped up and down with excitement; and then they ran into the garden, and Nana and Grandpa helped them up into the trees to collect their eggs.

And then the twins climbed into the tree house and looked at one egg after another. There were eggs like chocolate nests, with little eggs made of sugar inside. There were chocolate eggs packed with sweets: there were . . .

There were eggs of every kind!

And those they kept till last were made of cardboard, with pictures all over them of bright yellow chicks and Easter bunnies. Inside Michael's cardboard egg was a tractor for his toy farm: and inside Jenny's was the tiniest teaset on the tiniest tray, for her doll's house.

"So Nana didn't forget after all," said Mike.

"I think Nana and Grandpa think of the very best surprises in the whole world," said Jenny: but you couldn't quite hear all she said because she was taking the very first bite of her very first chocolate egg.

WHAT WE NEED IS A NEW BUS

Jean Chapman

Not so long ago an old red bus ran down to the station and back again. It was a rumbling-grumbling bus. It was a rusty-dusty bus. It was a jumping-bumping bus. And because it was all of these things some people walked to the station rather than ride in the old bus. It shook them about too much.

"The trouble with this old bus," the driver said, "is that it's worn out. It needs a new engine to drive it. It needs new tyres to run on. It needs new seats, new windows, new paint, new everything. In fact, what we need is a *new* bus!"

Now the bus wasn't surprised to hear this. It did feel worn out. It was worn out. Climbing the hills made its engine work so hard it went slower and slower and slower. Changing gears all the time made it feel exhausted. All it wanted to do was sleep in the sun for ever.

"*Ur, ur ur!*" it grumbled. It didn't want to go another wheel turn. Inside the bus the driver was in his seat in front of the big steering wheel. He pushed the gear lever into place. He pulled off the brake and before it knew what was happening the old red bus was rolling down the road again.

"*Urr-uuuuur*-urrrr-urrrrr!" It grumbled. It mumbled. It groaned. "*Grrr!*" It was as if it couldn't go another wheel turn. And to its surprise the old red bus didn't.

Sssss!

The front tyre was shrinking smaller and smaller. *Sssssssss!* What was happening to the plump round sides? *Sssssssss!* Air hissed out. The tyre was as flat as a piece of paper.

The driver stopped the bus. Out he jumped. People poked their heads from the windows.

"The front tyre is as flat as a pancake," the driver told them. "We can't fix it here. We need to get the mechanic from the garage," he said. "We could be here for hours. You'd better walk to the station."

Now the people grumbled and mumbled and groaned and moaned and walked to the station. "What we need is a new bus," they muttered and some of them stopped to look at the flat tyre that had run over a big nail. The nail had stabbed a hole in the tyre's tube. *Sssssss!* Out hissed the air until the tyre, no longer fat and round, looked saggy-baggy, as flat as flat. A sad limp tyre.

When, at last, the mechanic came roaring up in his truck he tapped the old red bus with a spanner and said, "This old crate needs more than a new tyre."

"I know, I know," agreed the bus driver. "What we need is a new bus. When can you sell us one?"

"Not today." The mechanic shook his head. He banged and tapped and looked at the insides of the bus and said nothing for a long time, then he said, "In a couple of weeks we could make this old bus almost as good as new, up at the garage."

Now that was a good idea. A wonderful idea, especially for the old bus. It helped as much as it could when the tow-truck came. There was a crane on the back of the tow-truck and it lifted the front wheels of the bus away, away off the ground. With just its two back wheels the old red bus ran along behind the tow-truck to the garage.

And when some people saw the old red bus being towed away they decided that it must be going to the scrap-heap. Where else could it go? "Looks as if we'll get a new bus after all," they told each other.

At the garage, mechanics took out the worn parts of the engine and put in new ones. They oiled and greased. They fitted new tyres and new seats. They repainted and repainted the old bus a sparkling red, a shiny red, a geranium red. It didn't look like an old bus. It didn't feel like an old bus. It felt like running a thousand miles or two – up hills, down hills and along lumpy, bumpy roads.

When the time came for the old red bus to drive along the road to the station everyone wanted a ride. They crowded in. Some people sat and some people had to stand. The bus was loaded but up the hill it went without a grumble or rumble, just a little *gr-grr-grrr* which was like a happy humming song. "This isn't bad for our old red bus!" said the driver with a grin.

"Not our old rumbling, grumbling bus!" shrieked someone. "This can't be our old, dusty, rusty bus! Don't tell me that this is the bumpy, jumpy, worn-out bus!"

It was, and we know that it was, don't we?

THE BLACK GEESE

Alison Lurie

L ong ago there lived a man and wife who had two children, a girl and a boy. One day the woman said to her daughter, "Elena, we are going to market today; stay in the house while we are away, and look after your baby brother, for Baba Yaga's black geese who steal children have been seen flying over the village. When we come home, we will bring you some sugar buns."

After her mother and father were gone, Elena stayed in the house with her brother for a little while. But soon she got tired of this, and took him outside to where her friends were playing. She put him down on the grass and joined in their games, and presently she forgot all about him and ran off. The black geese came down, seized the little boy, and carried him away.

When Elena came back and found her brother gone, she was very frightened. She rushed to look in every corner of the house and yard, but could not see him. She shouted his name, but he did not answer. At last she said to herself that the black geese must have stolen her brother and taken him to Baba Yaga, the terrible witch of the forest, who is eight feet tall and eats little children. "I must go after him," Elena said. And she began to run toward the forest.

She ran across the fields and came to a pond, and there she saw a fish lying on the bank, gasping for water.

"Elena, Elena!" it called. "I am dying!"

Elena wanted to hurry on, but she was sorry for the fish. So she picked it up and put it carefully in the pond, where it sank and then rose again to the surface. "As you have helped me, so I shall help you," said the fish. "Here, take this shell. If ever you are in danger, throw it over your shoulder."

Elena did not see how a shell could help her, but she did not want to seem rude, so she put it in her pocket and ran on. Presently she came to a grove of trees, and there she saw a squirrel caught in a trap.

"Elena, Elena!" it called. "My leg is caught!" Elena wanted to go on, but she felt sorry for the squirrel. So she released the trap. The squirrel darted up into a tree, and down again. "As you have helped me, so I shall help you," it said. "Here, take this walnut. If ever you are in danger, throw it over your shoulder."

Elena put the nut in her pocket and hurried on. Soon she came to a stony bank, and there she saw a field mouse trying to move a fallen rock.

"Elena, Elena!" it called. "I cannot get into my hole!" Elena was sorry for the field mouse, so she pushed and shoved until she had moved the rock aside. The mouse darted into its hole, and re-appeared. "As you have helped me, so I shall help you," it said. "Take this pebble. If ever you are in danger, throw it over your shoulder."

Elena put the pebble in her pocket, and ran on into

the dark forest, where the trees grow so close together that not a speck of sunshine can get through them. Soon she came to a clearing, and there she saw Baba Yaga's hut, which stands on three giant hens' legs and can move about when it likes. The black geese were roosting on the roof of the hut, a kettle was boiling on the fire, and Baba Yaga was asleep inside, snoring through her long nose. Near her on the floor sat Elena's little brother, playing with some bones.

Elena crept into the hut and picked up her brother. But as she ran away into the forest, the black geese saw her. They began to honk and to clap their wings, and Baba Yaga woke up.

"Stop, thief!" she screamed. "Bring back my dinner!"

Elena did not stop, or answer the witch, but hurried on with her little brother in her arms; and Baba Yaga came out of her hut and started after them on her long bony legs.

Elena could not run very fast, because her brother was too heavy. When she came out of the forest and looked back, she saw that the witch was gaining on them. What could she do? Suddenly she remembered what the fish had said, so she reached into her pocket and threw the shell over her shoulder.

At once a broad lake appeared behind her. It was too large for Baba Yaga to go around it, so she squatted down by the edge and began to drink. She drank so fast that the water began to sink at once, and it was not long before she had drunk up the whole lake. Then she ran on.

Elena looked back, and saw that the lake was gone and that Baba Yaga was gaining on them again. She remembered what the squirrel had said, reached into her pocket, and threw the walnut over her shoulder.

At once a thick grove of trees sprang up behind her. They grew so close together that Baba Yaga could not get through. So she began to chew up the trees with her sharp teeth. She ate so fast that in a few minutes she had eaten up the whole grove of trees. Then she ran on.

Elena looked back again, and saw that the trees were

gone, and the witch was coming after her again, so close
that she could hear her gnashing her long teeth and see
her reaching out her bony arms to grab them. She felt in
her pocket and threw the pebble over her shoulder.

Instantly a stony mountain sprang up behind her, so
tall that its top was lost in clouds. Baba Yaga could not
eat it or drink it; and she could not get over it. So she
had to go back into the forest, growling and cursing.

As for Elena, she went on to her village, and was safe
at home playing with her little brother when her father
and mother got back from market with the sugar buns.

RACHEL'S CAT

Alison Leonard

It was early morning. Rachel stood on tiptoe to look out of her bedroom window. She could see Gran's garden. There was grass first, then vegetables. If she tried hard, she could see next door's garden to the left. That was number 8, with lots of bright colours, which must be flowers.

If she looked the other way, to the right, there was the Higginses' at number 4. The Higginses had heaps of all sorts of things in their garden. Right at the end, they kept hens.

Rachel screwed up her eyes to see it all better.

Then she pulled on her T-shirt and jeans, and ran downstairs. She could smell breakfast. Gran was frying eggs, and burning the toast. Gran always burnt the toast. "Sure as eggs is eggs," she'd say, "I'll be burning your breakfast toast." "Eggs *are* eggs," said Rachel.

She sat down, scraped the burnt bit off her toast, and Gran slipped the egg on top. "It's my last egg," said Gran. "You'd best get round to the Higginses for some more, while I go and put my teeth in."

Rachel took two empty egg-boxes and went out into the garden. She knew the secret way through to the Higginses next door.

Where was the hole in the hedge? She was sure it was along here somewhere . . .

Something was running across the grass! What was it? It must have come from number 8. It looked like a streak of marmalade. Could it be a cat? Whatever it was, it had a long thick tail.

Quick as she saw it, it was gone.

She'd just found the secret way through to number 4, when . . .

Squawk – squeak – screech! Then – BANG! went the Higginses' back door.

Rachel saw Mr Higgins running down his garden. What on earth was he wearing? Something stripy, like pyjamas. Mrs Higgins was running after him. She wore something long, with a coat over it, and she was carrying another coat or something. Rachel crouched in the hole in the hedge, still clutching her egg-boxes, and peering.

"I'll get him!" shouted Mr Higgins as he disappeared towards the hen-run. Mrs Higgins stood shouting at him – "Harry! Harry!"

Rachel stayed crouching and peering. What was Mr Higgins talking about? Why was he so angry?

When Mr Higgins ran back, something horrid and limp and feathery was dangling from his hand.

He stopped. Rachel could see him now: he was glaring at her. "Well, young Rachel," he said. "Didn't you see it, then?"

"See what?" asked Rachel.

"That fox! In broad daylight. It got my hens! I saw the back of its tail just as it ran off. You must have seen it. Large as life!" And he stomped off back to his house.

"I only saw a cat," Rachel muttered. "At least I think it was a cat . . ."

"Never you mind," said Mrs Higgins. "It wasn't your fault. Oh dear! Our poor hens!"

Rachel crawled backwards into Gran's garden and ran back to the house. She told Gran the whole story.

Gran looked at her fair and square. "Rachel, my girl," she said, "I'm fetching you into town. You're going to have your eyes seen to."

Next day, they went in on the bus. In the middle of the main street was a boring sort of shop that Rachel hadn't noticed before. Gran said, "Here we are."

"Where are we?" asked Rachel. "What's this called?"

So Gran told her.

And the optician asked Rachel to look at all sorts of strange things: lights, and shapes, and pictures. She put

heavy spectacles on Rachel's nose, and little circles of glass in the slots. As each glass circle slotted into place in front of Rachel's eyes, the optician asked her, "Better or worse or not so good?"

Then they looked at frames. All different colours, all different shapes. Enormous ones like the round windows in a ship, tiny ones that made you look old-fashioned. There were even some exactly like Gran's.

Rachel chose some middle-sized frames with bright green edges. "Sure you want those?" asked Gran, frowning. "Sure as eggs is eggs," said Rachel. "Eggs *are* eggs," said Gran.

One morning, a week or so later, Rachel was pulling on her T-shirt and jeans when Gran called up the stairs. "Parcel for you, my girl!"

Screwing up her eyes to see what she was doing, Rachel tugged at the zip of her jeans. A parcel, for her? And it wasn't her birthday. She'd never had a parcel in her life before, except on her birthday.

It was lying on the kitchen table, wrapped in brown paper and covered in sticky tape. Rachel got her fingers tangled in the tape as she tore it open. Gran watched her, smiling all over her face.

It was Rachel's glasses, her new glasses, with their shiny lenses and their bright green frames.

"Put them on, then, girl," said Gran, impatiently.

It was like a miracle. She saw Gran. She saw the kitchen table with all the brown paper. Through the back door, she could see the garden with its grass first, then vegetables. She didn't have to screw up her eyes, and nothing was blurred.

All day, Rachel noticed things. A seagull's feathers. Green moss on the wall. Twigs on the top-most branches of the tree. Wispy evening clouds in the sky. The pattern on Gran's armchair when it was story-time.

Next morning, early, Rachel put on her new glasses, and stood on tiptoe to look out of her window.

She could see Gran's garden, and the neat flower beds at number 8. She could see everything in every heap in the Higginses' garden at number 4. She could even make out the wire round the hen-run at the far end.

Rachel smelt the breakfast that Gran was cooking in the kitchen downstairs: eggs frying, and toast burning. The eggs came from Mr and Mrs Higgins' new hens.

They'd bought them just the other day, and already the hens were laying eggs, brown and white, in the fresh straw beds.

Suddenly, Rachel saw something moving among the flowers of number 8's garden. What was it? It was ... moving marmalade. Slinky. Pointed nose, bright eyes. She could see the furriness of its long thick tail.

It was sliding towards the fence between number 8 and Gran's house, number 6. It might have been a cat – but it wasn't a cat!

"Gran!" shouted Rachel, and ran downstairs.

She rushed through the kitchen without stopping. "The fox!" she shouted. Gran dropped the fried egg sloshily back into the frying pan.

Rachel ran out of the back door, down the garden, and made straight for the secret hole in the hedge.

She ran up the Higginses' garden to their house, and banged on their back door. "Mr Higgins! Mrs Higgins! Come quick! It's the fox!"

Mrs Higgins, still in her nightie, opened the door. "What's up, then, Rachel?"

"Quick!" said Rachel, and ran back down the Higginses' garden.

She was near the secret hole in the hedge ... and

she stopped. There stood the fox. Rachel stared.

The fox stared back at her. She could see its dark shining eyes, and the white flash of fur at its throat.

Then it turned round, and slid away.

The Higginses ran up behind her, puffing. Mr Higgins had his jacket on over his blue striped pyjamas, and Mrs Higgins wore a brown coat over her nightie. Rachel turned round and said to them proudly, "It's all right! It's gone away. It won't hurt the hens."

"You saw it," said Gran, who was on her knees, crouching in the hole in the hedge. "You frightened it away."

"Yes, I saw it," said Rachel, grinning.

THERE'S SOME SKY IN THIS PIE

Joan Aiken

There was an old man and an old woman, and they lived in a very cold country. One winter day the old man said to the old woman,

"My dear, it is so cold, I should like it very much if you would make a good, hot apple pie."

And the old woman said, "Yes, my dear, I will make an apple pie."

So she took sugar, and she took spices, and she took apples, and she put them in a pie-dish. Then she took flour, and she took fat, and she took water, and she began to make pastry to cover the pie. First she rubbed the fat into the flour, then she made it into a lump with a little water.

Then she took a roller and began to roll out the pastry.

While she was doing this, the old man said, "Look out of the window, my dear, see, it is beginning to snow."

And the old woman looked out of the window at the snow, coming down so fast out of the white sky.

Then she went on rolling the pastry. But what do you think happened? A little corner of the sky that she had been looking at got caught in the pastry. And that little

81

bit of sky was pulled
under the roller, just the
way a shirt is pulled into the
wringer. So when the old woman rolled her pastry flat
and put it on the pie-dish, there was a piece of sky in
it! But the old woman did not know this. She put the
pie in the oven, and soon it began to smell very good.

"Is it dinner time yet?" said the old man.

"Soon," said the old woman. She put spoons and
forks and plates on the table.

"Is it dinner time now?" said the old man.

"Yes," said the old woman, and she opened the oven
door.

But what do you think? That pie was so light,
because of the bit of sky in it, that it floated out of the
oven, right across the room.

"Stop it, stop it!" cried the old woman. She made a
grab, and he made a grab, but the pie floated out of the
door, and they ran after it into the garden.

"Jump on it!" cried the old man. So he jumped on
it, and she jumped on it.

But the pie was so light that it carried them up into
the air, through the snowflakes falling out of the white
sky.

Their little black-and-white cat Whisky was in
the apple tree, looking at the snow.

"Stop us, stop us!" they called to
Whisky. So he jumped on to the pie.
But he was too light to stop it, and still

it went floating on through the falling snow.
They went higher and higher. The birds called to
them:

"Old woman, old man, little puss, so high,
Sailing along on your apple pie,
Why are you floating across the sky?"

And the old woman answered,
"Because we can't stop, that's the reason why."
They went on, and they came to a plane that
had run out of fuel. So there it was, stuck, in
the middle of the sky. And the airman was inside,
and he was very cold. He called out,

"Old woman, old man, little puss, so high,
Sailing along on your apple pie,
Why are you floating across the sky?"

And the old woman answered,
"Because we can't stop, that's the reason why."
"May I come with you?" called the airman.
"Yes, of course you may."
So he jumped on the pie and went floating
along with them.
They went a little farther and they saw a
duck who had forgotten how to fly. So there
it was in the middle of a cloud. And the duck
called,

"Old woman, old man, little puss, and airman,
    so high,

Sailing along on your apple pie,
Why are you floating across the sky?"

And the old woman answered,
"Because we can't stop, that's the reason why."
"May I come with you?"
"Yes, of course you may."
So the duck jumped on the pie and went floating along with them.

They went a little farther and they passed a tall mountain. On the tip-top of the mountain was a mountain goat, who had forgotten the way down. So he called to them,

"Old woman, old man, little puss, and airman, and duck, so high,
Sailing along on your apple pie,
Why are you floating across the sky?"

And the old woman answered,
"Because we can't stop, that's the reason why."

"May I come with you?"

"Yes, of course you may."

So the goat jumped on the pie too.

Then they went a little farther and they came to a big city with high, high buildings. And on top of one of the buildings was a sad, cross, homesick elephant, looking sadly and crossly at the snow. She called to them,

"Old woman, old man, little puss, and airman,
   and duck, and goat, so high,
Sailing along on your apple pie,
Why are you floating across the sky?"

And the old woman answered,

"Because we can't stop, that's the reason why."

"Your pie smells so warm and spicy, it makes me think of my homeland," said the elephant. "May I come with you?"

"Yes, of course you may."

So the elephant jumped on to the pie and they went floating on. But the elephant was so heavy that she made the pie tip to one side.

Now as they floated on, by and by they left the cold and the snow behind, and came to where it was warm. Down below was the blue, blue sea, and in the blue sea were many little islands with white sand and green trees.

By this time the pie was beginning to cool off, and as it cooled it went down and down.

"Let us land on one of these lovely islands," said the old man. "They have white sand and green trees, and ever so many flowers."

"Yes, let us!" said the old woman, and Whisky the cat, and the duck, and the mountain goat, and the airman, and the elephant.

But the people on the island saw them coming and put up a big sign that said NO PARKING FOR PIES.

So they went a little farther and they came to another island. But the people on that island also put up a big sign that said NO PARKING FOR PIES.

"Oh dear," said the old woman, "will no one let us land?"

By this time the pie was so cool that it sank down on the sea.

"Now we are all right," said the old man. "Our own pie makes a very fine island."

NO PARKING FOR PIES

NO PARKING FOR PIES

NO PARKING FOR PIES

"There are no trees!" said the old woman. "There are no flowers! And what shall we eat, and what shall we drink?"

But the sun was so warm that fine apple trees soon grew up, with green leaves, and pink flowers, and red apples. And the mountain goat gave them milk, and the duck gave them eggs, and Whisky the cat caught fish in the sea. And the elephant picked apples for them off the trees with her trunk.

So they lived happily on the island and never went home again.

And all this happened because the old woman baked a bit of sky in her pie!

THE PAPER PALACE

Paul Biegel

Caroline had a bad leg and it kept her in bed for a long time. She was fearfully bored, because she had read all her books and used up all her paints.

Then her grandmother bought her a present. A nice present: a pair of scissors.

"For my nails?" asked Caroline.

"No," said Grandmother. "To cut things out of paper."

"What kind of things?" asked Caroline.

"People," said Grandmother. "And animals and trees and houses and anything you can think of."

It was not at all easy. First Caroline cut out a car, but it looked more like a jam jar on legs. Then she made a hare and a rabbit, but they looked more like funny hats.

She took a new sheet of paper and cut out another animal.

"Did *you* make that dog?" her father asked. "With your grandmother's scissors? Jolly good!"

89

Caroline practised and practised and after a week she could cut out anything she liked with the scissors. Even little houses, which she would cut out and then stick together. Everyone had heard about it and everyone in the neighbourhood came to look. There was the farm which sick little Caroline had made, with barns and stables and chickens and cows and pigs. And ducks, in a silver paper pond.

"Good gracious, Caroline, how clever!"

One night Caroline had a strange dream. A tiny little man, smaller than her little finger, skipped onto the table. "You must make a palace," he said.

"A palace?" asked Caroline. "What for?"

"For the queen," said the little man. "In three days' time she is giving a party and it's got to be in a beautiful new palace."

"Made of paper?" asked Caroline.

"Naturally," said the little man. "And you must cut it out. With a big ballroom and two kitchens with stoves and a broad staircase to the upper rooms and turrets with flags and battlements and parapets and a double front door with a flight of steps. And you must make footmen too, and cooks and dancing girls. Lots of dancing girls, because it's going to be a big party."

Caroline had to laugh about it next morning, and yet she could not forget her dream. "You know," she thought, "I'm really going to make it. A whole palace. For my own pleasure."

She began to snip and stick and stick and snip. Walls with windows in them, turrets with battlements, the ballroom floor, the steps leading upwards.

"What are you making, Caroline?" her mother asked.

"Oh, a palace."

By evening she had stuck two walls together and part of the stairs.

That night she dreamed of the little man again. He tripped across the ballroom and gave the walls a push which made the paper crackle. "Is it really sturdy enough?" he asked.

"Yes, of course," said Caroline.

"And where are the kitchens?"

"I've still got to do them," said Caroline.

She made the kitchens the next day and the upper rooms with the broad staircase leading up to them and the turrets with flags on them.

"You'll have to hurry up," said the little man on the third night of her dream. "You've only got one day left. What about the flight of steps? Where are the cooks and footmen and dancing girls? And one of the towers must be higher."

Caroline began immediately after breakfast. She cut out twelve dancing girls and stuck them on one leg in a circle round the ballroom. She cut out seven cooks on two legs by the stoves in the kitchens. She stuck an extra bit on the tower and made the steps and two big trees for the outside.

"Marvellous, child. Marvellous," said her mother. "Shall I put it away now?"

"On the table," whispered Caroline.

But that night Caroline did not dream. No, she woke up instead. A light was shining in the room, a strange white light. She turned her head and then she saw it. In the middle of the table her paper palace stood sparkling and glittering as if a thousand lamps were burning inside it. Music was pouring from the windows and shadows were moving against the transparent paper walls – the shadows of people dancing.

"The party!" thought Caroline. She was longing to sit up, but her bad leg wouldn't let her.

Then the people in the palace started to sing and clap their hands and laugh and shout hooray and "Long live the Queen!" and Caroline saw the shadows of skipping, swaying, leaping and whirling people dancing across the white walls.

Then she looked at the tall tower. There at the top stood the little man of her dream, on guard.

"Hallo!" Caroline called to him.

At that very moment everything fell dark and silent.

How strange, thought Caroline, and next morning she thought again: how strange. Of course it was only a dream, but it seemed just as real as if I were awake.

"I say, how strange," her mother was saying, as she set the castle beside Caroline's bed. "I didn't remember that you had put a little man on the tower as well."

93

Caroline's eyes opened wide. "It wasn't a dream," she whispered.

"What do you mean?"

But Caroline didn't answer. She peered with one eye through the window into the ballroom. And there, in the middle of the dance floor, inside the ring of twelve dancing girls on one leg, stood another figure, in a wide cloak and with a crown on her head: the queen.

And when the neighbours said, "You did cut out *that* one cleverly, she's so real it looks as if she were alive," Caroline would say, "I didn't make that one."

But no one believed her.

THE GOOSE AND HER LITTLE IRON HOUSE

Italo Calvino

Once upon a time there was a gaggle of geese who were on their way to a part of Italy called the Maremma to lay their eggs. When they were half way there, one of them stopped and said, "My sisters, I shall have to lay my egg right away. I cannot wait until we get to the Maremma. But you must go on all the same, without me."

"Surely you can wait!"

"Hold on to it for a little longer."

"Do not leave us!"

But there was nothing to be done. The little goose simply had to lay her egg. So they embraced each other, said goodbye and promised to see each other again on their way back.

The little lone goose went off into a wood. There she made a nest of dry leaves at the foot of an old oak tree and laid her first egg. Then she decided to go for a walk to find some fresh grass and clear water for her dinner.

She got back to her nest as the sun was setting but the egg had gone. The next day she had the idea of going up

95

into the oak tree to lay her second egg among the branches, thinking it would be safe there. When she came down from the tree she was feeling quite happy and set off in search of something to eat, just as she had done the day before. When she returned, the egg had disappeared.

The little goose thought to herself, "There must be a wolf in the wood who is stealing my eggs."

She went to a nearby town and knocked at the door of the blacksmith.

"Mr Blacksmith, could you make me a little house of iron, please?"

"Yes, if you will lay a hundred pairs of eggs for me."

"All right, put a basket down just here and, while you make the little house for me, I will lay the eggs for you."

So the goose settled down and, at every hammer blow that the blacksmith struck as he worked on the little iron house, she laid an egg. When the blacksmith had struck the two hundredth blow with his hammer, the little goose presented him with the two hundredth egg and hopped out of the basket.

"Mr Blacksmith, here are the hundred pairs of eggs I promised you."

"Mrs Goose, here is your little house, all finished."

The little goose thanked him, put the house on her back, carried it through the wood and set it down in a field.

"This is just the place for my goslings," she said to herself. "There is fresh grass to eat here and a stream to bathe in." And, very pleased about everything, she shut herself inside so that she could lay her eggs in peace at last.

While all this had been happening, the wolf had returned to the oak tree but there were no more eggs. He started searching in the wood until he found himself in the field and there he came across the little iron house.

"I am certain that little goose is inside," he thought to himself and knocked at the door.

"Who is it?"

"It is me, the wolf."

"I cannot open the door for you. I am sitting on my eggs."

"Little goose, open the door."

"No. If I do, you will eat me."

"Take care, little goose. If you do not open the door right away –

"I will climb on your roof,
I will dance on your roof,
I will do the fandango
And your house will fall, bang-o!"

And the little goose replied:

"You may climb on my roof,
You may dance on my roof,
You may do the fandango
But my house will not fall, bang-o!"

The wolf leapt up onto the roof and, pit-a-pat, pit-a-pat, started to jump about this way and that. But, sure enough, the more he jumped about, the more solid the house of iron proved to be. The wolf got very cross indeed. He jumped down and ran away while the little goose nearly burst her sides laughing at him.

The wolf did not come again to the field for several days, but the little goose was always very careful to lock the house properly whenever she went out. By now her eggs had all cracked open and a lot of baby goslings had hatched out.

One day, there was a knock at the door.

"Who is it?"

"It is me, the wolf."

"What do you want?"

"I have come to tell you that the fair is being held tomorrow. Shall we go there together?"

"By all means. What time will you come and fetch me?"

"Whenever you like."

"Then you can come at nine o'clock. I cannot be ready before that as I must care for my little ones first."

And they said goodbye to each other like good friends. The wolf was already licking his whiskers, quite sure that he would soon be eating the goose and her goslings in two mouthfuls.

But the next morning the goose got up at dawn, gave the goslings their breakfast, kissed them all and told them on no account to open the door to anyone. Then she locked the door behind her and went to the fair.

It was just eight o'clock when the wolf came knocking at the little iron house.

"Mummy is not here," said the goslings.

"Open the door!" ordered the wolf.

"Mummy does not want us to open it."

The wolf said to himself, "I will eat you later," but aloud he said, "How long is it since your mother went out?"

"She left early this morning."

The wolf, without waiting to hear more, ran off at a great rate. The poor little goose had finished her shopping and was returning home when she saw the wolf coming towards her very fast, with his tongue lolling out.

"Where can I hide to save myself?" She had bought a large soup tureen at the fair. She put the lid of the tureen on the ground, settled herself on top of it and pulled the dish right over herself, upside down.

The wolf stopped in his tracks. "Well, just look at that fine monument! I must put some flowers on it!" He picked a great bunch of flowers and placed it in front of the soup tureen and started off again.

The little goose cautiously put her head out and looked around. Then she gathered up the flowers, picked up the soup tureen and set off for home and the warmth of her goslings all round her once more.

Meanwhile the wolf was at the fair, looking everywhere for the goose. He even looked under all the stalls but could not find her anywhere. "As I did not meet her on the road, she must still be here," he thought to himself and started his search all over again.

The fair was over, the stall-holders were packing up all the goods they had not sold and taking down their stalls. But the wolf could still find no trace of the little goose. "She has got the better of me again!" he thought.

Half dead with hunger, he went back to the little house of iron.

"Who is it?"

"It is me, the wolf. Why did you not wait for me?"

"It was very hot. And, besides, I thought I would meet you on the road."

"But which road did you take?"

"There is only one."

"So how could we have missed each other?"

"I saw you. I was inside the monument."

At this the wolf became very angry. "Little goose, open the door for me at once."

"No, because you would eat me."

"Take care, little goose –

"I will climb on your roof,
I will dance on your roof,
I will do the fandango
And your house will fall, bang-o!"

And the little goose replied:

"You may climb on my roof,
You may dance on my roof,
You may do the fandango
But my house will not fall, bang-o!"

Pit-a-pat and pit-a-pat! But however much he jumped

about, the house of iron proved to be stronger than ever.

The wolf did not put in an appearance for several days. But one morning there was a knock at the door.

"Who is it?"

"It is me, the wolf. Open up!"

"I cannot, I am busy."

"I came to tell you that it will be market day on Saturday. Do you want to go with me?"

"By all means. Call for me as you are passing."

"Tell me exactly what time you want me to call for you, so that the same thing does not happen as when the fair was here."

"Let us say at seven o'clock. I cannot be ready before that."

"That suits me," and they left each other like good friends.

When Saturday morning came, the goose got up before daybreak. She smoothed the goslings' feathers, gave them some fresh grass, told them not to open the door to anyone and set off. It was just six o'clock when the wolf arrived. The goslings told him their mother had already left and he ran off to catch up with her.

The little goose was standing in front of a melon stall when, in the distance, she saw the wolf approaching. There was no time to escape. Seeing a big round melon on the ground, she made a hole in it with her beak and climbed inside.

The wolf slunk round and round the market in search of the little goose. "Perhaps she has not arrived yet," he said to himself, and went to the melon stall to choose the best one for himself. He took a bite out of one and tasted another but threw them away, for their skins were too bitter. At last he noticed a particularly large, round one on the ground. "This must surely be a good one," and he took a bigger bite out of it than he had taken out of the others. The little goose, who was inside and whose beak happened to be just by the place where the wolf had bitten, saw a little window open up in front of her and she spat straight out of it.

"Pah! Pah! It is horrible!" exclaimed the wolf, giving the melon a push that set it rolling. He did not see where it went. It rolled down a steep slope and split open against a stone. The little goose sprang out and ran all the way home.

After searching in every corner of the market until the sun went down, the wolf went to the little house of iron and knocked on the door.

"Little goose, you did not keep your word. You did not go to the market today."

"Oh yes, I did. I was there all right. I was inside that big, fat melon."

"So you have tricked me again! Now open the door!"

"No, because you would eat me."

"Take care, little goose –

"I will climb on your roof,
I will dance on your roof,
I will do the fandango
And your house will fall, bang-o!"

And the little goose replied:

"You may climb on my roof,
You may dance on my roof,
You may do the fandango
But my house will not fall, bang-o!"

Pit-a-pat, pit-a-pat, but the house of iron did not even shake as the wolf pranced about.

Some time passed. One day the wolf came back, knocking at the door once more.

"Come along, little goose, let us make peace between us. Let us eat a fine supper together so that we may forget the past."

"By all means, but I have nothing to offer you that would suit your taste."

"I will look after that side of things. You just see to the cooking and the setting of the table."

So the wolf started to come and go, bringing now a salmon, now a soft cream cheese, now a hard cheese, now a chicken – all things he had stolen from the neighbourhood. Soon the little iron house was crammed full of good things to eat.

The day fixed for the supper arrived. The wolf had eaten nothing for two days so that he would have a bigger appetite – but, as you can imagine, he was not thinking of any of the succulent things he had brought, but of the delicious tender mouthfuls of goose and gosling he would soon be having.

Off went the wolf to the house of iron and called out, "Little goose, are you ready?"

"Yes, when you want to come, everything is ready. But you must somehow manage to squeeze in through the

window. The table is so laden that it fills the whole room and I cannot open the door."

"It is all the same to me. I am ready to come up to the window."

"I will throw down a rope to you. Thread your tail through the loop and I will pull you up like that."

The wolf, who could hardly wait to eat the little goose, threaded his tail through the loop and was instantly tied fast. The more he tugged, the more he kicked his legs about, the more the slip-knot tightened and the more he spluttered. The little goose was pulling him up, higher and higher, when, just as the wolf's tail reached the window-ledge, she suddenly let go. Down he fell to the ground, stone dead.

"Come along, my little goslings," she said, as she opened the door. "Come and eat some nice fresh grass and have a swim in the stream."

At last it was safe for the

goslings to come out of their house. They had a fine time, flapping and flipping their wings and chasing each other all over the place.

One day, the little goose heard the beating of wings and the sound of birds calling. It was the time of year when the geese return from the Maremma. "If only they were my sisters!" she thought to herself.

She went to the road and saw a gaggle of geese flying towards her, with all their goslings coming along behind. They made a great fuss of each other, as good sisters should, and the little goose told them about her adventures with the wolf. The sisters liked the iron house so much that they all went to the blacksmith and asked him to make one for each of them.

And even now, in some fields (I am not sure where), there is a whole village of little iron houses where geese live quite safe from wolves.

THE LIMP LITTLE DONKEY

Judy Bond

Peter's donkey was a limp little donkey, a saggy, thin little donkey, a floppy old donkey. He was knitted from grey wool, with red and green stripes round his middle, and little brown feet. He no longer had enough stuffing to make him stand up, or sit up, or even lift up his head!

Peter liked to have the limp little donkey in bed at night, but when morning came, Peter would be off to play. Mother would find the donkey under the blankets when she came to make the bed.

She would try to prop him up, and *try* to prop him up, but he couldn't stand, or sit, or even lift up his head. He could only lie with his legs going all ways. In the end, Mother would leave him on his back on top of the cupboard, and there he'd have to stay.

One day, someone gave Peter a new, golden teddy bear. That night Peter took *him* to bed and forgot his limp little donkey.

The donkey was left lying on top of the cupboard. "I wish I were a big strong toy! I wish someone would play with me. I wish I could stand up, or sit up, or even lift up my head to see what is going on," he said to himself.

Nothing changed. Weeks and weeks went by, and no one played with the limp little donkey. He stayed on top of the cupboard, a dusty, forgotten little donkey.

Then Peter's brother brought home a puppet he had made at school – such a funny fellow, dressed like a clown. He was very limp too, with dangling wooden arms and dangling wooden legs. He had pieces of string tied to each ankle and wrist, and whenever the strings were pulled, he danced.

"We're going to have a puppet show," said Peter's brother. "We'll get all the toys and dolls and put strings on them too."

Peter's brother made a stage out of boxes and old curtains, and he hid behind it and made the clown dance. He tried to make the dolls and the teddy bear dance too.

"It's no use," he said. "They're too stiff. Where's that limp little donkey?"

So the limp little donkey came down from the top of the cupboard. Strings made from black cotton thread were tied to his four legs and to his neck too. Then he was put on the stage where everyone could see him. Peter's brother pulled the black cotton strings, and oh – oh –

Up came the donkey's head! It nodded from side to side.

Up came his legs. They kicked this way and that.

"Look at me! Look at me!" he cried to the other toys. "I can stand, I can sit, I can even lift up my head – and I *can dance*! Dance, dance, *dance*!"

Peter laughed and clapped his hands. The limp little donkey was the best puppet of all!

When the puppet show was over and Peter was going to bed, he said, "Come along, little donkey. Where have you been all this time?"

The limp little donkey, the saggy, thin little donkey, the floppy old donkey cuddled up happily between Peter and the golden teddy bear, and was soon fast asleep.

THE HUNGRY BUNYIP

Virginia Ferguson

Long ago, in the Australian bush, there lived a farmer and his wife and a bunyip. The bunyip was their pet, and they kept him in a shed at the back of the house. The man liked food and so did his wife – but you should have seen the bunyip eat! This is what he had for breakfast:

four meat pies with sauce,

three saucepans of porridge,

two buckets of milk,

and one sack of ripe apples.

By the end of the day there wasn't a scrap of food left in the house. The man and his wife grew thinner and thinner, while the bunyip ate them out of house and home.

"I think he'll have to go," said the farmer.

The next morning, the bunyip met the farmer and his wife filling a bucket of water near the windmill.

"Good morning, Farmer. Good morning, Wife."

"Good morning, Bunyip. Have you eaten yet?"

"Yes, but I'm still hungry," said the bunyip. "I've only had:

four meat pies with sauce,

three saucepans of porridge,

two buckets of milk,

and one sack of ripe apples . . .

so if you don't mind, I think I'll eat you, too."

He opened his mouth and gobbled up the farmer and his wife. Then he ran to the cowshed where the cow was mooing, waiting to be milked.

"Good morning, Cow," said the bunyip.

"Good morning, Bunyip. Have you eaten yet?"

"Yes, but I'm still hungry," said the bunyip. "I've only had:

four meat pies with sauce,

three saucepans of porridge,

two buckets of milk,

one sack of ripe apples,

and the farmer and his wife . . .

so if you don't mind, I think I'll eat you, too."

He opened his mouth and gobbled up the cow.

In a cloud of dust a drover rode up on his horse, followed by a whole herd of cattle.

"Good morning, Drover."

"Good morning, Bunyip. Have you eaten yet?"

"Yes, but I'm still hungry," said the bunyip. "I've only had:

four meat pies with sauce,

three saucepans of porridge,

two buckets of milk,

one sack of ripe apples,

the farmer and his wife,

and the cow . . .

so if you don't mind, I think I'll eat you, too."

He opened his mouth and gobbled up the drover, his horse and the whole herd of cattle.

A flock of sheep was standing by a tree full of kookaburras.

"Good morning, Sheep. Good morning, Kookaburras."

"Good morning, Bunyip. Have you eaten yet?"

"Yes, but I'm still hungry," said the bunyip. "I've only had:

    four meat pies with sauce,

    three saucepans of porridge,

    two buckets of milk,

    one sack of ripe apples,

    the farmer and his wife,

    the cow,

    and the drover, his horse and his whole herd of cattle . . .

so if you don't mind, I think I'll eat you, too."

He opened up his mouth and gobbled up the sheep and the tree full of kookaburras.

The bunyip came to a school.

"Good morning, Children," said the bunyip.

"Good morning, Bunyip," sang the children. "Have you eaten yet?"

"Yes, but I'm still hungry," said the bunyip. "I've only had:

four meat pies with sauce,
three saucepans of porridge,
two buckets of milk,
one sack of ripe apples,
the farmer and his wife,
the cow,
the drover, his horse and his whole herd of cattle,
and a flock of sheep and a tree full of kookaburras . . .
so if you don't mind, I think I'll eat you, too."

"Eat the teacher first," cried the children.

So the bunyip opened his mouth and gobbled up the teacher.

"Hurrah!" shouted the children. But then he gobbled them up as well.

A shearer's cook saw this happen. The bunyip didn't like the look of the angry cook.

The cook yelled, "What made you do such an awful thing? Why did you eat the teacher and a whole school of children?"

"I was hungry," cried the bunyip.

"Hungry?" roared the cook. "What have you eaten today?"

"Not very much," cried the bunyip, trembling with fright. "I've only had:

four meat pies with sauce,

three saucepans of porridge,

two buckets of milk,

one sack of ripe apples,

the farmer and his wife,

the cow,

the drover, his horse and his whole herd of cattle,

a flock of sheep and a tree full of kookaburras,

and a teacher and a whole school of children . . ."

"Well, don't think you can eat me, too," said the shearer's cook. "Why don't you try a billy of my special shearer's stew?"

He heated the stew but the bunyip didn't see him put in half a bucket of pepper.

"Open wide," said the shearer's cook, and he poured it down the bunyip's throat.

People in a town far away thought a cyclone was coming. All the thunderstorms in the world couldn't sound as loud as the sneezes which came from the bunyip's burning nose.

Ah choo! – and out jumped the schoolteacher and the whole school of children.

"Finish your work before you go out to play," she said.

Ah choo! – out flew the tree full of kookaburras.

Ah choo! – out leapt the flock of sheep.

Ah choo! – out rode the drover on his horse, droving his herd of cattle.

Ah choo! – out jumped the cow, still mooing to be milked.

Ah choo! Ah choo! – and out shot the farmer and his wife.

The farmer's wife milked the cow, the farmer went off to work on his farm, and everyone lived happily ever after.

But the bunyip was never seen again.

LITTLE PIG AND THE HOT DRY SUMMER

Margaret Gore

A re you sitting comfortably? Then I'll begin.
"I wish it would rain!" said Little Pig.

There had been no rain for weeks and weeks, and all the pigs were puffing and grunting with the heat. In the field beyond the pigsties the ground was as hard as an overbaked cake.

No rain meant that there was no mud. And what Little Pig loved most of all was mud. Thick, squelchy, oozy *mud!* Little Pig would roll on his back, waving his four pink trotters in the air and squealing with delight.

"If *only* it would rain!" sighed Little Pig. "This summer has been so hot and dry, and I *do* love a mucky roll in the mud!"

In the sty next door to Little Pig lived Big Pig. Big Pig was a terrible boaster.

"I could make it rain – if I *wanted* to, that is," he said. None of the other pigs believed Big Pig. Especially Quick Pig, who had a sharp tongue.

Quick Pig said, "Go on then, *make* it rain, Big Pig!"

"I – I don't think I have time just now," replied Big Pig.

Slow Pig grunted, "He knows he can't, that's why."

Big Pig pretended to be busy rooting about for something to eat. Slow Pig had hardly moved all summer – except to eat. He just lay by the wall, snoring. Even Kind Pig, who was a most patient pig, grew tired of Slow Pig's snoring.

The weather grew hotter and hotter. And *still* no rain.

"I don't think I shall ever have a good, mucky roll in the mud again!" wept Little Pig.

"Of course you will, Little Pig," said Kind Pig. "I'm sure it must rain soon!"

And it *did* rain. That very night.

First came a few big spots. Splash, splash, splodge. Then it rained faster and faster, and heavier and heavier.

Now it was simply bucketing down! The rain hissed on the roof; it swept across the yard; it gushed down the drains.

It made a noise like a hundred pigs all drinking at once from a high trough!

But the trouble was, now that the rain had started it wouldn't stop. It went on all the next day, and all the next night, and all the next day after that!

"It's never going to stop raining!" squealed Little Pig. Quick Pig blamed Big Pig.

"*You* made it rain – and now you can't stop it!"

"It's not *my* fault," grumbled Big Pig.

There was water everywhere. Even the field became a lake. The ducks from the pond were able to swim right up to the wall of the pigsties. *Inside*, the pigs were huddled together, squealing; and *outside* the ducks swam up and down teasing them, and laughing their quacky laughs.

The water got higher and higher. Little Pig was frightened, but Kind Pig said, "Don't cry, Little Pig. Look, here is someone coming to save us."

It was Tom the farmhand. He came sailing across the field on a wooden raft which he had just knocked together from an old door.

Tom put down a plank from the pigsties on to the raft, and then the pigs walked across it. First Quick Pig – because he was always first with everything (especially eating!).

Then Big Pig, because he had knocked everyone else out of the way. Then Kind Pig, who showed Little Pig how to walk along the plank without falling off, and lastly Slow Pig – it *had* to be Slow Pig didn't it!

The pigs sailed away on their raft, to a dry place on the other side of the field. And there they had to stay, until, next morning, they were awakened by Little Pig squealing and squealing.

"Wake up, wake up," cried Little Pig. "The sun's shining, and all the water has gone! We can go home."

Little Pig was quite right. They did go home, but not by raft, because there was no water left. They had to go by tractor, because the whole field was a mass of – MUD.

"Squelchy, oozy, delicious MUD!" cried Little Pig. When they reached home, the pigs trotted happily back into their own sties. First Quick Pig, then Big Pig, then Kind Pig, and last of all, Slow Pig.

But where was *Little* Pig?

The pigs crowded to the wall and looked over into the field.

There was Little Pig. He was lying on his back in the mud, waving his four pink trotters in the air and squealing with delight.

"I *do* love a good mucky roll!" said Little Pig.

THE GREAT SUPERMARKET TROLLEY RACE

Edward Blishen

This happened one day when Kate went into the supermarket with Mum. It was the day after her fourth birthday. (Don't forget that!) She'd had a great party and had eaten three LARGE bowls of strawberry jelly. Kate knew she'd eaten three LARGE bowls of strawberry jelly, but nobody else knew it. One was the bowl of jelly she was supposed to have eaten. One had been given to her by her friend Dan. Dan didn't like jelly. The other she'd found in the kitchen after the party. She had tried quite hard not to eat this bowl of jelly. But it looked as if it badly wanted to be eaten. And she badly wanted to eat it. And no one was there to see what she did. So she ate it.

(Remember! She'd eaten three quite LARGE bowls of strawberry jelly!)

And there was Kate, on the day after her birthday, with her mother in the supermarket. You know how it is in supermarkets – you go down one row, and that's perhaps meat and fish and things. And you go up another, and that's crackly popply things for breakfast.

They'd gone up the row where you went for tea and coffee. And now they were in the row where they kept the milk and butter and cheese.

What happened then would have made Kate's hair stand on end, but she'd had it cut short for her birthday. If it had stood you wouldn't have known. But her heart went bang bang BANG.

Because a supermarket trolley was coming towards her, and it was travelling at enormous speed.

Twenty miles an hour, she thought. And then she thought: *That's* not twenty miles an hour! *That's* sixty miles an hour!

Kate shut her eyes and waited to be knocked down and squashed flat. But just before she shut her eyes she saw a quite old lady standing on the back of the trolley. She was steering it. She was shouting, and Kate thought she was waving her hat. She was looking very cheerful. Then there was a tremendous whoosh. Kate opened her eyes and saw the trolley had gone. From the sound it made she knew it had turned the corner on two wheels.

And at her feet was the quite old lady's hat. It must have fallen out of her hand as she went whizzing past.

Then she heard a great roar coming from the other direction. It was another trolley. And this one must be going at eighty miles an hour. It was being steered by an old gentleman. He had a wrinkly face, and was smiling broadly. It was a white smile, because he had very white teeth. And he was wearing a helmet, and that was as white as his teeth. It was like the helmets racing drivers wear. The old smiling gentleman was making his trolley weave from side to side. In his hand he had a sort of . . .

What was it?

A sort of . . . high-powered thing. A sort of . . . long metal pole with . . . sort of hands at the end of it. He was using it pick up things as he went flashing past. A quick stab of the pole – press a button! – the hands open! – the hands shut! – and that was a pot of yoghurt! Same again, but the other side – that was a packet of cheese! And back to the first side – press the button! – hands open! – hands shut! – that was a tub of icecream! Into the trolley with them and – scream! screech! squeal! – he'd gone round the corner, too. If you could go round the corner on one wheel, not even two, that's what he'd done.

"Mum, what's *happening*?" cried Kate.

Now, Kate's mum is a jolly mum. But Kate had never seen her looking so jolly as she did now. She had leapt up on the back of her own trolley, and that too had begun to roar and race. Her eyes were gleaming! Her hair was streaming behind her.

"Jump on, Kate! Jump on!"

Somehow she managed to land inside the trolley. The speed was amazing! Round the corner they went. Mum had one of those poles with the mechanical hands, and she was tossing apples and oranges and lettuces and bananas into the trolley. Most of them missed Kate. But she was hit by a bunch of grapes, and accidentally swallowed one or two. That pleased her, because she liked grapes, and they were seedless.

"Mum!" she cried above the roar of the trolley wheels. "What's happening? It wasn't like this in here last week!"

"I know," shouted her mother. She threw back a melon that she'd picked up by mistake. "I think it must be because there's a new manager," she said. "It's a race. That's what they say. First one back at the checkout is the Supermarket Trolley Champion of the Year!"

Round the next corner they passed one or two accidents. Trolleys had crashed into one another and overturned. Their wheels were spinning helplessly. No one seemed to be hurt. The drivers were lying on the supermarket floor, laughing wildly. The quite old lady was lying there, too, and seemed to be laughing more wildly than the rest. There were little pools of smashed eggs, and a great litter of broken biscuits.

And my goodness, Kate was proud of her mum! After that mistake with the melon, she didn't make another. For a time she was neck and neck with a lady with red hair. This lady's husband was steering the trolley. He had no hair at all. She kept shouting at him: "Step on the gas!" But then Kate and her mother had flashed past her, and were tearing after other trolleys they could see ahead of them.

"*Chocolate!*" cried Kate as her mother raced past the sweets. To her amazement her mother did a perfect U-turn. With her pole she snatched *two* bars of chocolate instead of one. She said, "Oh bother!" but didn't wait to throw one back. (Kate was delighted!) Then she turned the trolley again and once more dashed after the leaders.

And one after another, she overtook them. There was one lady who tried to ram their trolley, but she was no match for Kate's mum, who put on a stupendous turn of speed and dodged out of the way.

They were in the last row, the one with bottles and cans.

And now Kate could see the checkout ... the manager standing beside it ... a flag held high in the air.... Then they had reached it, the flag had fallen: they had won!

THEY HAD WON!

Their names would be in the papers! They would be on television! They would be given a great silver cup! They would open a huge bottle of whatever that drink was that fizzed! And Kate would hold the bottle and make it fizz!

They were the Supermarket Trolley Champions of the Year!

But suddenly they weren't.

Because Kate was in bed. It was the night after the party. (I hope you haven't forgotten about the jellies!) She was lying there and shouting at the top of her voice: "We've won! We've won!"

And her mother was running into the room.

So Kate stopped shouting.

Her mother asked her what had woken her up. And when Kate told her, she asked one or two more questions.

Which was how she got to know about Kate having eaten three LARGE bowls of jelly.

"If you don't want nightmares, Kate, you shouldn't eat too much jelly," she said.

Kate saw what she meant. But she wasn't sure that it counted as a nightmare. She'd enjoyed it.

I'm sorry to tell you that once or twice since then she has secretly tried eating three (once, it was *four*) bowls of jelly. But it didn't work: the trolleys in the supermarket never again went more than . . .

Well, as Kate worked it out, only a measly bit more than nought miles an hour!

'FRAIDY MOUSE

Anne Wellington

O nce upon a time there were three grey mice, and they lived in a corner of a barn.

Two of the mice weren't afraid of anything, except the brown tabby cat who lived in the farmhouse. Two of the mice said, "Hi! Look at us. We're tricky and we're quicky and we're fighty and we're bitey. We're not afraid of anything, except the tabby cat."

But the third little mouse said, "Don't look at me. I'm afraid of everything. I'm a 'Fraidy Mouse."

'Fraidy Mouse's brothers said, "Don't be ridiculous. There's nothing to be frightened of, except the tabby cat."

'Fraidy Mouse shivered, "I've never seen a tabby cat. Does Tabby Cat stamp with his feet? Does he growl?"

'Fraidy Mouse's brothers said, "Don't be absurd. Tabby Cat sits by the door of the barn.

He sits on the ground,
He's big and he's round.
He doesn't move a muscle
Till he hears a little rustle.
Then he'll jump. Thump!
And he'll eat you till you're dead."

Then 'Fraidy Mouse's brothers said, "But Tabby Cat's indoors now. So off we go together to be bold, brave mice."

'Fraidy Mouse was left alone, sitting in the barn. In case he should see something fearsome and frightening, he closed his eyes tightly and fell fast asleep.

While 'Fraidy Mouse was sleeping, the farmer passed the barn. He was carrying a sack full of big brown potatoes. One of the potatoes fell out and rolled about. It rolled to the door of the barn. And there it stayed.

'Fraidy Mouse woke up. He saw that big potato. "Mercy me! It's Tabby Cat, sitting by the door!

He's sitting on the ground,
And he's big and he's round.
He won't move a muscle
Till he hears a little rustle.
Then he'll jump. Thump!
And he'll eat me till I'm dead."

'Fraidy Mouse kept so still that all his bones were aching. Then his brothers came back, and they said, "Hi, 'Fraidy Mouse!"

'Fraidy Mouse whispered, "Hush! Oh hush! Don't you see the tabby cat sitting by the door?"

'Fraidy Mouse's brothers said, "Don't be idiotic. That's not a tabby cat. That's a big potato." And they laughed. 'Fraidy Mouse's brothers rolled around laughing, until they were exhausted and had to go to sleep.

But poor little 'Fraidy Mouse cried himself to sleep.

While the mice were sleeping, the farmer passed the

barn. He picked the potato up and carried it away. 'Fraidy Mouse twitched in his sleep – dreaming. He dreamed he was a tricky, quicky little mouse.

As the sun went down, the big brown tabby cat came padding to the barn. And he sat by the door. 'Fraidy Mouse twitched in his sleep again – dreaming. He dreamed he was a fighty, bitey little mouse.

After a while, the mice woke up. The first thing they saw in the twilight was the cat, a big round brown thing sitting by the door. 'Fraidy Mouse's brothers hid away in holes. They stared out with frightened eyes, too terrified to speak.

'Fraidy Mouse thought they were teasing him again, pretending to be frightened of a big brown potato. He wouldn't get caught like *that* again!

He called out, "Hi there! You silly old potato!" The tabby cat was so surprised he didn't move a muscle. 'Fraidy Mouse called again, "I'm only small and 'Fraidy. But I'm not afraid of *you*, you silly old potato. And neither are my tricky, quicky, fighty, bitey brothers."

Tabby Cat said to himself, "What a mouse! If that's a little 'Fraidy Mouse, the smallest, most afraid mouse, his brothers must be terrible. I shan't come here again."

Then Tabby Cat stalked away, pretending not to hurry. And 'Fraidy Mouse said, "Funny! That potato's got a tail!"

'Fraidy Mouse's tricky, quicky, fighty, bitey brothers came creeping from their holes, and they said, "Oh, 'Fraidy Mouse! How brave you were to talk to the tabby cat like that!"

'Fraidy Mouse thought, "Tabby Cat! That wasn't a potato. I was talking to a real live tabby cat. Oh my!"

Then his legs gave way, and he fell on his back. And his brothers said, "He's resting. It's tiring being so brave!"

MRS MOPPLE'S WASHING LINE

Anita Hewett

Mrs Mopple was a farmer's wife, and on Monday morning she did her washing. "Now what have we got today?" she said to herself.

"A frilly pink petticoat
A pair of woolly bedsocks
Two white gloves
And a red spotted handkerchief."

Mrs Mopple finished her washing and pegged it on the clothes line alongside the cabbage patch to dry. "There!" she said. "Blow wind, blow."

Then the wind blew strongly over the cabbage patch. Mrs Mopple's Monday wash fluttered on the line like flags in a row.

The frilly pink petticoat
The pair of woolly bedsocks
The two white gloves
And the red spotted handkerchief.

140

Mrs Mopple went indoors, because she was going to get the dinner for herself, her husband, the pig, the turkey, the chicken, the jersey cow, and the rabbit.

Blow wind, blow. It blew so strongly that snap! went the pegs that were holding the petticoat. The frilly pink petticoat tossed in the air, twice round the haystack and over the farmyard. Then down it came on the little black pig, tight round his little black middle. The pig sat down in the middle of the farmyard.

So there he was
A pig in a petticoat.

Blow wind, blow. It blew so strongly that snap! went the peg from one woolly bedsock. The bedsock went tossing into the air, twice round the haystack and over the farmyard. Then down it came on the gobbly red turkey, tight on his head like a warm woolly nightcap. The turkey sat down in the middle of the farmyard.

So there they were
A pig in a petticoat
A turkey in a nightcap.

Blow wind, blow. It blew so strongly that snap! went the peg from the other woolly bedsock. The bedsock went tossing into the air, twice round the haystack and over the farmyard. Then down it came on the little yellow chicken, tight round her neck like a winter woolly muffler. The chicken sat down in the middle of the farmyard.

So there they were
A pig in a petticoat
A turkey in a nightcap
A chicken in a muffler.

Blow wind, blow. It blew so strongly that snap! went the pegs that were holding the gloves. The two white gloves tossed in the air, twice round the haystack and over the farmyard. Then down they came on the jersey cow, tight on her horns with their fingers sticking upwards, like eight white finger-horns and two white thumb-horns. The cow sat down in the middle of the farmyard.

So there they were
A pig in a petticoat
A turkey in a nightcap
A chicken in a muffler
A jersey cow with ten horns.

Blow wind, blow. It blew so strongly that snap! went the pegs that were holding the handkerchief. The red spotted handkerchief tossed in the air, twice round the haystack and over the farmyard. Then down it came on the grey fluffy rabbit, tight all over him spotted like the measles.

The rabbit sat down in the middle of the farmyard.

So there they were
A pig in a petticoat
A turkey in a nightcap
A chicken in a muffler
A jersey cow with ten horns
A rabbit with the measles.

So there they were!

Mrs Mopple came out of the kitchen, and as she came she said to herself: "Blow wind, blow. The wind has blown my washing dry."

Mrs Mopple looked at the clothes line, and as she looked she said to herself: "Blow wind, blow. The wind has blown my washing *off*."

Mrs Mopple looked at the farmyard, and she blinked her eyes. And as she blinked she said to herself: "Blow wind, blow. What do I see?

"A pig in a petticoat
A turkey in a nightcap
A chicken in a muffler
A jersey cow with ten horns
A rabbit with the measles.

I don't believe it,
I don't BELIEVE it."

Mrs Mopple went indoors to tell Mr Mopple. *He* didn't believe it either. Do you?

THE LITTLE DRAGON AND THE SNOWMAN

Iris Smith

The little dragon peered out from the castle porch at the snow-covered garden.

"What's this?" he said. He took a step out, but jumped back quickly when his long-clawed foot sunk into the cold wet snow.

The princess laughed at him and ran out into the garden.

"I love snow!" she shouted as she threw handfuls of it into the air.

The little dragon, who had followed her out, was not so sure. He did not like the way it squelched through his toes when he walked. He hated the way it tickled his back when it fell on his scales. He particularly disliked the sizzling sound it made when big snowflakes settled on his warm nose.

"It's lovely, it's lovely!" shouted the princess. "I'm going to make a snowman."

"Humph," grunted the little dragon, and a puff of smoke escaped from his nose.

"Humph," he grunted again and turned back towards the castle. He slipped and slithered down the snow-covered path until he reached the porch. He wished that he was a big dragon so that he could blow nice warm flames instead of little puffs of smoke. He crawled into a corner away from the wind, wrapped his long scaly tail round his feet and looked sadly out at the snow. He hated cold weather.

The princess was having a lovely time. She was building a snowman – a big one with a large fat body and a perfectly round head.

"Come and look," she called to the little dragon.

The little dragon shook his head and shuffled backwards further into the archway.

"Oh, do come on," demanded the princess.

Reluctantly the little dragon crept out and picked his way through the snow. He looked at the snowman. The snowman looked back.

"Humph," said the little dragon and walked around the snowman. He sniffed the snowman's feet and he licked the snowman's hand, but the snowman did not move. The little dragon tipped his head on one side and looked carefully at the snowman. The snowman smiled.

"Hallo," said the little dragon happily, and he smiled a very strange dragon smile back at the snowman.

"It's time for tea now," called the princess as she ran down the path towards the castle.

"What about the snowman?" asked the little dragon.

"You can't take a snowman indoors," yelled the princess. "Leave him there – and do come on!"

The little dragon did not want to leave the snowman out in the cold, but he had to obey the princess so he followed her back into the castle. He was not allowed into the dining room where the princess had her tea so he went down the passage to the kitchen.

It was warm inside the kitchen and the little dragon soon forgot about the snowman. He ate the bowl of warm stew that the cook had made for him. Then he curled up on the warm rug in front of the fire. Soon he was fast asleep and dreaming.

When he woke it was not yet morning. Everyone was in bed and the palace was quiet. The fire had gone out and the little dragon shivered in the cold night air. It reminded him of how cold it had been out in the snow. Then he remembered the snowman.

The poor snowman – out in the freezing cold! The little dragon went down the passage, through the big door and out into the garden.

It was cold! It was freezing! Huge icicles hung from the trees and the frosted leaves sparkled in the moon-light. The frozen snow crunched when the little dragon walked on it. In the middle of the ice-cold garden the snowman stood all alone with the smile still on his face.

"Come indoors," said the little dragon, taking the snowman's hand. The snowman did not move.

"Where's your legs?" asked the little dragon, peering at where the snowman's body met his feet. The snowman did not answer.

"Never mind, I'll push you," said the little dragon cheerfully. He pushed and pushed until the snowman came unstuck from his piece of ground and slid slowly down the path. The little dragon gave one last huge push and the snowman was over the doorstep and inside the castle. Down the passage they went and into the kitchen.

"You'll soon be warm," he said, carefully wrapping a blanket round the snowman. Then he curled himself up in a corner and went back to sleep.

He was woken by the screams of the cook.

"What's all this water?" she shouted, as she rushed around banging buckets and brooms.

The little dragon opened his eyes and looked around him. A huge puddle was spreading fast and in the middle of it the snowman stood with the blanket still round him. The little dragon looked again. Something was wrong with the snowman. He had lost his smile – and he was smaller! The little dragon was sure that he had been bigger than that when he had been brought inside.

"What's all this noise?" shouted the princess as she ran down the stairs into the kitchen. "How did that get in here?" she asked, pointing to the snowman.

"You!" the princess and the cook shouted together as they turned to face the little dragon. "You brought it in."

The little dragon hung his head.

"I told you to leave the snowman out in the garden. They like being cold. Warmth makes them melt," added the princess.

The little dragon was sad. He had only wanted to help the snowman. He sighed and huge tears ran down his cheeks and sizzled on his nose.

The princess patted his head gently. "Now don't cry," she said. "Help me get the rest of the snowman outside – then we can have breakfast."

Later that day the little dragon watched from the porch as the princess rebuilt the snowman. When it was finished, the little dragon crept out to say how sorry he was, but he soon went back to the nice warm kitchen. And the snowman stayed smiling in the cold.

HARRY AND THE LADY NEXT DOOR

Gene Zion

Harry was a white dog with black spots. He loved his neighbours, all except one.

He did not love the lady next door. The lady next door sang. She sang high and loud. When she sang, Harry's ears hurt.

She sang louder than the siren on the fire engine. When she sang, the firemen put their hands over their ears.

She sang higher and louder than the cats. When she sang, the cats ran away.

Harry tried everything to make her stop. He howled under her window. His friends howled too. But it did no good. The lady next door went on singing. She sang higher and louder than ever.

One day Harry's family gave a party. They invited the lady next door. When she started to sing, Harry almost bit her leg. But he bit the leg of the piano instead.

The family sent Harry out of the room.

"You're a bad dog," they said. Harry just wagged his tail.

As he walked out some people said, "Poor Harry." Others whispered, "Lucky dog!"

When Harry pushed the door open the wind blew in. It blew pages of music off the piano, all around the room. Everyone tried to catch them but nobody could.

The pages blew out of the door into the garden. They blew over the fence into the trees. Harry caught some of the pages but he didn't bring them back.

He ran until he came to a quiet spot. He dropped the music and lay down.

Soon he fell asleep.

Then something woke Harry up. All around him were cows mooing. They mooed very low notes. Harry listened. He thought the cows made beautiful music.

He had never heard anything so soft and low. He wished the lady next door would sing like the cows.

Suddenly Harry had an idea.

He barked at their heels. Down the road they went. Harry barked and the cows mooed.

They ran on and on, down the main street, past the school, the library and the fire station.

At Harry's house the lady was still singing. Harry stopped the cows. They mooed and mooed and mooed. They mooed soft and low. The cows mooed for a long time but it did no good. The lady next door went on singing. She sang higher and louder than ever.

Harry's family called the man who owned the cows. He took them home.

That night, Harry slept in the dog house.

The next day the lady next door sang again. Harry's ears hurt more than ever. He went for a walk. After a long time he heard a wonderful sound.

"Oompah! Oompah! Oompah! Oompah!"

It was low and lovely.

Then Harry saw what it was. It was the big horn in the brass band. It was even softer and lower than cows mooing. Harry wished the lady next door would sing like the big horn.

Then he saw the leader of the band. The leader threw his stick into the air.

Suddenly Harry had an idea.

The next time the stick went up, Harry caught it. Harry ran in front of the band. The leader ran after Harry – and the band ran after the leader. Soon the leader was out of breath. He stopped. But the band ran after Harry. They played as they ran.

Harry led them down the main street, past the school, the library and the fire station. Harry stopped the band in front of the lady's house. She was still singing.

The big horn player played even softer and lower. He blew and blew and blew right under her window. But it did no good. The lady next door sang higher and louder then ever.

When the leader got there, Harry gave the stick back.

That night, he slept in the dog house again.

A few nights later, the family took Harry to the park to hear the brass band. They knew Harry liked the big horn. They got to the park and sat down. The people were quiet. They waited for the music to begin. Harry closed his eyes.

He waited for the big horn. But the low notes never came. Instead, a man came out.

"Good evening, friends," he said. "The band won't play tonight. The big horn player has run out of breath. Instead, we'll have a singing contest. And here are the ladies who will sing."

Everyone clapped when the ladies came out. At the back was the lady next door. Harry took one look and ran off. He was almost out of the park when he heard:

"Blurp Blurp."

"Blurp Blurp."

It was low and beautiful. Harry stopped and listened. It was even softer and lower than the cows and the big horn. He wished the lady next door would sing like this.

Then he saw where the sound came from. It came from inside a watering can.

Suddenly Harry had an idea.

He took the handle of the can in his mouth, and ran with it. When he got back to the bandstand, he walked quietly up the stairs. The lady next door was singing. Harry put the watering can on the floor behind her.

Soon the lady sang a *very* high note.

Then something happened. Two frogs jumped out of the can. One jumped on the lady's head. The other jumped on her shoulder. The other ladies in the contest shrieked and ran away.

But the lady next door went on singing, higher and louder than ever. When she finished her song, everyone shouted, "Hooray!'"

The judges whispered together. Then one of them spoke.

"Ladies and gentlemen, the other ladies have gone home. So the lady next door wins the singing contest! She is a *brave* lady. She wins first prize. She can study music in a far-off country for a long time!"

Everyone clapped and clapped. Harry barked and barked. He was the happiest of all.

In the middle of all the fuss the frogs hopped home.

Soon the time came for the lady next door to go away. Harry went to the ship with the family to see her off.

"Goodbye! Goodbye!" everyone shouted.

Harry wagged his tail.

The lady next door started to sing a goodbye song. But no one heard her. Just as she sang the first note the ship blew its foghorn. It was a deep, low, wonderful sound. As the ship moved away other boats blew their foghorns too.

Acknowledgements

For permission to reproduce copyright material
acknowledgement and thanks are due to the following:

A M Heath & Co Ltd for 'There's Some Sky in This Pie' from
A Necklace of Raindrops copyright © Joan Aiken, 1968
(Jonathan Cape Ltd); the author for 'Little Dog Turpie' from
Folk Tales copyright © Leila Berg 1966 (Brockhampton
Press); Penguin Books Ltd for 'The Paper Palace' from *The
Elephant Party and Other Stories* copyright © Paul Beigel 1973
(UM Holland-Harlem), English text copyright © Penguin
Books 1977; Methuen Children's Books and A M Heath &
Co Ltd for 'The Thin King and the Fat Cook' from *Time and
Again Stories* copyright © Donald Bisset 1970;
the author for 'The Limp Little Donkey' copyright © Judy
Bond 1983 from *Stories to Share* (Hodder and Stoughton
Australia); J M Dent & Sons Ltd for 'The Geese' by Italo
Calvino copyright © Guilio Einaudi editore s.p.a. 1956 &
1972, English translation copyright © J M Dent & Sons Ltd
1975; the author for 'What We Need is a New Bus' copyright
© Jean Chapman 1978; Faber and Faber Ltd for 'Horace'
from *The Stories of Horace* copyright © Alice B. Coats 1987;
Methuen Children's Books for 'My Naughty Little Sister
Goes to the Pantomime' from *My Naughty Little Sister*
copyright © Dorothy Edwards 1952; Hutchinson Children's
Books for 'Little Pig and the Hot Dry Summer' copyright ©
Margaret Gore 1984 from *Animal Tales from Listen With
Mother*; The Bodley Head for *Mrs Mopple's Washing Line*
copyright © Anita Hewett 1966; David Higham Associates
for *The Little Brute Family* copyright © Russell Hoban 1966
(Pan Books Ltd); the author for 'A Bed for Tiny Ted'
copyright © Margaret Joy 1976; Walker Books Ltd for 'One
Very Small Foot' from *Sophie's Snail* copyright © Dick King-
Smith 1988; William Heinemann Ltd and HarperCollins